SC
Sec   Second Sight

DISCARD

second sight

second sight

stories for a new millennium

- madeleine L'engle
- richard peck
- avi
- natalie babbitt
- janet taylor lisle
- rita williams-garcia
- nancy springer
- michael cadnum

Philomel Books ■ New York

Book design by Semadar Megged. The text is set in 12.25-point Granjon.
Library of Congress Cataloging-in-Publication Data
Second sight : stories for a new millennium / Avi . . . [et al.].   p.   cm.
Summary: A collection of short stories by such authors as
Madeleine L'Engle, Richard Peck, Rita Williams-Garcia,
and Nancy Springer.
1. Children's stories, American.   2. Short stories.   [1. Short stories.]
I. Avi, 1937–   .   PZ5.S4375   1999   [Fic]—dc21   99-15218   CIP
ISBN 0-399-23458-6
3 5 7 9 10 8 6 4

contents

•

Oswin's miLLenNium

■ a v i

two days before the end of the world
Oswin woke with a start. In the tim-
bered stable where he slept, winter's frost
was further chilled by the ashen glow of a cold
morning moon. The smell of rotting straw was
strong. The stench of manure stronger still.

In haste, Oswin felt himself all over, clotted
hair to dirty toes, as well as the filthy wool
tunic that covered him from neck to knees. He
even examined his soil-encrusted hands and
grimy fingers. Ten being the highest number
Oswin could count, he was satisfied all his dig-

its were there, proof he had survived another day. The great red dragon with the seven heads and ten horns had yet to come. Satan, in the form of a serpent, had not arrived. Nor had the world begun to burn.

Oswin sighed. Two more days until the millennium. He might still have some hope of salvation.

In haste he got to his feet and peered around the stable at the four oxen. The beasts were standing in their stalls, eyes closed, jaws working, just as if everything was normal.

The oxen were Oswin's best friends. Indeed, except for Brother Godwin, they were his only friends. Eleven years ago, when Oswin's parents had been killed during a Viking raid, Oswin, still an infant, had been handed over to the Abbey St. Benedict. Though the boy survived, he was truly a slave, knowing nothing but work from morning till night throughout the year. No payment for his labor. The stable for shelter. A bit of food.

Of late there had been times Oswin had allowed himself thoughts of running away. Father Godwin had encouraged it, told him of a great village by a great river, London by name, where a boy might hide. But now, with the year 1000 at hand and the imminent return of Jesus Christ—the monk was certain of that—there was little reason to break the law by going off. The wrath of Bodo the farm steward would be great. God's wrath would be worse.

The thought brought Oswin to his knees. Fairly bursting with fear, he began to pray earnestly, acknowledging his many sins. Laziness, stupidity, and curiosity were the things he was usually accused of. In his prayers he begged the Lord for forgiveness. But oh, he thought with agony, how could I, a wretched boy, even dare to hope for salvation? Surely, it's nothing I can do on my own.

Oswin found his sandals, tied them on, and hurried to his tasks. The end of the world or no, he had work to do. Bodo would make sure of that. And yet, for the boy, even a flogging from the steward seemed preferable to the multitude of horses that were approaching, horses with serpent tails, lions heads, from whose mouths belched fire, smoke, and brimstone. Just to think of them brought a cold sweat to his brow. As for the floods and the earthquakes that were also due to erupt, Oswin could not begin to imagine them.

The boy poured water into the oxen's trough, then pitched them hay. The hay, alas, reminded him of the sickle hanging on the wall. He stole a fleeting glance at it and shuddered. What was it that Father Godwin had said? "When God arrives, He will have a sharp sickle in his hand to cut sinners down. Then He will crush their souls in a wine press until their blood gushes forth. Harken to me, boy: with the coming of the millennium, only the pure in heart shall find life after death."

How Oswin wished he could get it all out of his mind!

The constant fear kept his stomach a hard knot. He knelt again and prayed with new fervor. Only then did he set about cleaning the stalls.

Two hours later, when his stable work was done, Oswin stepped outside. Though the moon was fast fading, dawn had not arrived. Just enough light existed to make the snow patches luminescent and the hoarfrost on the twisted, leafless oak trees glitter like old bones.

Oswin's stomach gurgled. Surely, the boy thought, to feel hungry, when in two days time he would be altogether beyond food, was yet another sin.

Burdened with guilt and shame, Oswin looked to the hill top. There were flashes of light as the abbey monks, candles in hand, passed along the columns in the side aisle of the church. The rhythmic thrum of their chant kept step with a drum that beat like a heart.

The boy's own heart filled with grief. Here the world was about to end, but the monks remained steady in their prayers. If he had anything to give, Oswin would have given it all to be so calm. How he envied the monks' ability to be so sure of themselves.

Deeply unhappy, Oswin started up the frozen path that led to the long-timbered house where many of the other serfs lived. There in the kitchen, not far from where the chickens were kept, he would break his fast, and hope no one would notice him. If they did they might abuse him— spitting on him, beating him—as they so often did. There were times Oswin was quite certain that in all the world he was the least of the least.

As the boy walked he resumed his prayers—as Father Godwin had taught him—keeping his eyes focused upon the ground. Then he spied a human skull. It gave him a terrible shock. Only when he looked a second time did he realize it was not a skull, but a rock. The shadowy light of dawn had made it appear different. But had not Father Godwin taught Oswin that the world was full of mystic signs—if one could only read them?

Wanting to be sure it was a rock, Oswin approached it cautiously. Extending a foot, he tapped it over. Beneath the rock was a frog.

Oswin started back with terror. Father Godwin had told him that when the world ended, frogs would come out of the mouths of dragons. Could this frog be one of those?

The frog hopped away into the bushes.

Forgetting break fast, forgetting his field work, the boy tore up the rutted pathway toward the abbey. When he reached it, he went to the kitchen doors.

Like Oswin, Father Godwin had been a foundling. Though some said he was smart, he was not liked by the other abbey monks. "He thinks himself high and clever," was the common complaint. Throughout life—and he had lived almost all of it at the Abbey St. Benedict—Father Godwin had been in the kitchen. "Thou thinkist thyself too wise, too knowing," the abbot had scolded him sixty years ago. "A life in the kitchens will tutor thee in humility." He was still there.

The old monk and the young boy had come to know each other because, twice a week, it was one of Oswin's tasks to bring eggs to the kitchen.

To his great relief Oswin found Father Godwin in the kitchen yard, flinging slops onto the refuse piles.

He was a small, stooped man with the thick hands and features of a peasant. Teeth long gone, his mouth had collapsed. His eyes were pink, constantly runny. There were more lines on his face and his hands then on a thatched roof. His brown cassock was decrepit, tied at his waist with a bit of frayed rope. Thin, white, tonsured hair crowned his pate. He had told Oswin that, by his own careful reckoning, he was two hundred years old. The boy did not doubt him.

As soon as Oswin saw the monk, he went on his knees in the courtyard mud.

"Father Godwin, Father Godwin," he cried.

"Ah, my wretched boy, what ails thee today?" the old man said, hobbling to him.

"Father," Oswin cried, "I uncovered a frog."

"Did thee boy?" the old man returned with solemnity. "Was it a . . . *live* one?"

"It was, Father. It hopped away. And here it's already winter. There should be no frogs."

"Ah, another sign," the old monk sighed.

"Could it have come from a . . . a dragon's mouth?" asked Oswin.

"Very good," the old man said with a teacher's pride. "Thou hast remembered the Revelations well. Yes, it must have been exactly that. But harken to me now," he said in the low voice of a conspirator, "I have gone over my reckoning. Methinks I've made a mistake."

"A mistake, Father?" Oswin said, peering up into the old man's face. The boy was still on his knees.

"As I have told thee, boy, by my figuring, the living shall come to judgement at the hour of midnight, at the end of this, the Year of Our Lord, 999. When midnight arrives it becomes the year 1000. As clearly prophesied in the Revelations of Saint John the Divine, it bringeth the second coming. The end of the world is neigh."

Oswin, hands clasped tightly, faced turned up, eyes fairly glued to the ancient face, nodded. "Yes, Father, I understand."

"I have informed the abbot," Father Godwin went on with some bitterness, "but he mocks me. Calls me a blockhead. So be it. He ignores the truth at his own soul's peril. But thee, my son, thou doth believe me. And thus, for thee, there remains hope."

"I do believe thee, Father, I do. But . . . but thee said there was a mistake."

"So I did. I told thee that the apocalypse would be in three days time."

"Thou did so, Father, and I have been praying constantly."

"Well," the old man continued, "mine eyes are old. Methinks I did not do the numbers proper."

"And . . . ?" Oswin said, feeling the stirring of hope.

"It is *not* two days from now that the world shall end. It will be . . . tomorrow."

"Tomorrow!" Oswin gasped.

"At the stroke of midnight. And boy, thy frog doth prove it mightily."

"Please, Father," Oswin begged with tears in his eyes. "can I do nothing about it?"

"Pray, my son," was the answer. "Pray and beg for forgiveness. So that when the angel of the Lord comes—like a thief as the Book says—and empties his vial upon the earth, thou may not be covered with grievous sores."

"But . . . but my voice is so very small," Oswin wept. "How can my prayers be heard by the mighty Lord?"

"Do not be of such little faith, boy," the old man said kindly. "Thou hast a great heart. But perhaps I should pray for thee."

Oswin snatched up the ragged, muddy hem of the monk's cassock and kissed it fervently.

"Would thee?" he cried. "Oh, would thee?"

"I could. But . . ."

"Yes, Father?"

"I would like an offering," the monk said wistfully.

"Whatever I can do, Father, I'll do. I promise."

"Very well." Pursing his lips, the old man grew thoughtful. "Yes, I would like thee to bring me . . . an egg."

"An egg?" Oswin repeated, not sure he understood.

The old man's eyes sparkled. "A round, plump egg. The kind the abbot devours for his dinners. He maintains the egg is perfection itself. So before the world ends to-morrow, I, for once in my mortal life, should like to eat something which is perfect, an egg."

"But . . . but where can I get thee one?" Oswin asked.

"Doth not thee carry eggs from the farm steward twice a week to this kitchen?"

"Yes, Father. Master Bodo gives them to me to bring."

"Well then, fetch one and bring it to me now. Here. I shall wait for thee."

"But . . . but . . ."

"Boy, the world ends tomorrow. Locusts the size of horses are flying toward us even now. They have faces like men, the teeth of lions, tails with scorpionlike stingers to stab sinners like thee and me. Surely I might have *one* egg."

"Is . . . is it not a sin to steal?"

"Thee and I are so laden with sins, boy, one more shall make only a jot of difference. But without my prayers, I fear thee shall be thrown into the bottomless pit with the beast whose name is Apollyon."

"I . . . I will get an egg, Father," Oswin said in haste.

"Do so and I will pray for thee. In the meanwhile, I

shall return to my calculations and see if I can be more precise as to time of the millennium. Methinks that if we had the name of the Lord in our mouths at the very moment of doom, it would bring salvation. Now, off with thee!"

Bowing clumsily, Oswin turned and fled from the abbey, hastening back to the stables. There, panting, sides aching from his hard run, he flung himself on his straw pile, crying from the sheer terror of the situation. And when the pinching cold began to claw deep into his bones, he burrowed himself even deeper in the straw.

The truth was, the thought of stealing an egg was very frightening to Oswin. If he were caught there was no telling what Bodo would do to him. Better to run off. "Ah, but what good is that?" he wept. Could anything the steward do be worse than what would happen to him—when the world ended?

But if he did filch the egg, and Father Godwin did pray for him, surely God would listen and spare him. In short, to commit the sin of theft might be his only hope.

Then Oswin had a further thought: Perhaps if he warned Bodo about what was about to happen, the steward, to save himself from the smoke, fire, and torments, might *give* Oswin an egg. Yes, that was the better way. It was his last, best chance.

Stomach growling with hunger, Oswin returned to the path that led to Bodo's house. As he went, he took notice of the skull-like rock. In full daylight it looked nothing like that now. But . . . was that too an omen?

The main farm building was built of large timbers with wattling between. The thatched roof, like a great hummock of hay, seemed heavy under the now gray skies.

Oswin went to the rear of the house. The front door was forbidden to slaves. Instead, he clumped through the rear yard, sinking ankle deep in soggy muck and mire. There was a well and a chicken roosting shed, which he glanced at, but dared not approach.

Though the backdoor of the house was open, he stood on the threshold and only peered inside. The kitchen was dim, the sole light coming from a hearth that held a small wood fire. It made him think of hell fire.

"Yes, boy?" a voice demanded. It was Dame Mildred, Bodo's wife. A large woman, she had a perpetually red face and corpulent arms and hands, which she was quick to use.

"Thou art sorely late," she scolded. "What ails thee?"

"I was delayed, mistress," Oswin replied, not daring to look up. Dame Mildred always called him a saucy boy and liked to box his ears at the most trifling provocation.

"And if I were to detain thy break fast, thou would find yourself ill used, I'm sure."

"Yes, mistress."

She reached into a box, pinched up a piece of stale black bread and handed it to him. "The break fast wine is gone," she said. "Thou can have some at eve."

Oswin took the bread bit gratefully. "And if it pleases thee," he murmured, "Master Bodo. May I speak with him?"

"About what business?"

"A . . . a request from the abbey."

"Fie on thee! They will speak to him directly, I'm sure. He is there now and due home soon. Now get thee gone. Do thy labor."

Bowing, Oswin backed into the yard. Once there, he put the bread to his mouth. Though hard and small, it was bread. He gnawed at it gratefully.

As he ate, he tried to decide what to do. There was work to be done in the fields. The oxen needed to be exercised. It would go poorly with him if he did not do his work. But here it was, almost . . . tomorrow.

A chicken strutted by, clucking, pecking in search of seeds. Oswin eyed it with envy.

The chicken made its way into the small roosting shed. Oswin looked around guiltily, made sure that no one was about, then followed.

The roost was foul smelling even to Oswin's nose. Dung and feathers clung from floor to ceiling. The two dozen birds, alarmed by the boy's presence, squawked loudly on their shelves. These shelves, full of straw, were their nesting places.

In a panic that the noise would bring Dame Mildred, Oswin groped frantically about the straw until his fingers found a smooth lump. He drew it out and held it in the palm of his hand. It was an egg. Should he or should he not take it? What if he were seen? Suddenly the chickens reminded him of one of the four beasts that stood guard before God's throne. As Father Godwin had revealed to him, one of these beasts was like an eagle, except that it had six wings. And it was *full* of eyes—whatever that meant—that never closed.

Oswin drew his hand—and the egg—into his tunic and stepped into the yard. He was half way out when Bodo, the steward, appeared.

Bodo was a large, swarthy man, who wore his cloth cap low over his small, ratlike eyes. His nose was large, his mouth never quite closed, exposing stained, gaped teeth. He had a habit of clenching and unclenching his massive hands.

Boy and man stared at each other.

"Villain, what art thee doing here?" the steward roared. "And why are there feathers on thee?"

"I . . . I . . ."

But before Oswin could say anything, the livid steward was on him, grabbing and shaking him, feeling over Oswin's tunic. It took but a trice before he detected the egg.

Taking it up, Bodo smashed the egg against Oswin's face. Its' contents dribbled down.

"Thief!" Bodo cried, "I shall teach thee to steal from me!" He dragged the unprotesting boy to the well where a bucket of cold water was standing by. The man picked the bucket up with one hand, and emptied it over Oswin, soaking him. Then he cuffed him a few times about the head and face. Finally, he hauled him to a wood shed, yanked open its door, thrust the boy inside, slammed shut and latched the door. "Stay there till I fetch thee!" he shouted.

Shivering from the freezing water as well as emotion, feeling more alone than he had ever felt in his whole miserable life, Oswin sank back against the piles of wood and wept bitterly.

In time he stopped crying and wiped the egg from his face. Though hungry, he was afraid to taste it. It was not, he knew, meant for the likes of him.

In his chest his heart felt like a stone. His one chance of saving himself had been lost. What would happen to him now? More beatings? More isolation? Less food? It was impossible for him to think he could be under any greater torment than that which he was currently suffering.

Then and there it was as if Oswin's heart broke: His sole consolation was that tomorrow, when the world ended, it would be a relief.

Let it happen, he thought to himself. I don't wish to live anymore. "Forgive me, God," he murmured out loud, "I am the worst of the worst, thy greatest sinner. I deserve whatever happens to me."

Oswin was not let out of the shed until the end of day. Nor was it Bodo who released him, but his wife, Dame

Mildred. Pity was not the motivation. She was in search of firewood.

"Get thee hence!" she shouted at the boy, drawing him out and shoving him away. "Thee are no longer wanted here."

Oswin did not even dare ask for his supper bread.

Instead, in the desolate winter twilight, he made his weary way back to the abbey. The distant, steady chanting of the monks could not soothe him. He had failed, not just himself, but his only human friend, Father Godwin. By so doing he had lost his sole chance of salvation. Before the night was over, he would be cast into the fiery pits of hell. So be it.

He tapped upon the abbey door. A monk, unknown to Oswin, answered his timid summons. He was a tall, thin fellow with a beak of a nose. "What doth thee want, boy?" He was not so much unkind as he was disinterested.

"Father Godwin, if it pleases thee."

"Father Godwin? He's off in a pother about his foolish apocalyptic calculations."

"I'll wait, if it pleases."

"As thee wishes," the monk said, and went away.

Shivering, Oswin remained by the door. Now and again he stamped his feet and beat himself about with his arms.

As it grew colder, as night came, he gazed up at the heavens, certain he had never seen so many stars. They sparkled brightly through his trickling tears.

Oswin was sure he had waited so long it was close to midnight. Father Godwin, the boy assumed, was never coming. But Jesus Christ was, and the end of the world was imminent and he was all alone. Exhausted, he decided to return to the stables. At least the oxen would welcome him.

And indeed, the four beasts were hungry and thirsty. Oswin hurried to provide straw and water. Then, pulling his knees up to his chest, he sat in their stall. Where it was warmest. What will happen will happen, he told himself, too weary to pray. I care not. I cannot be more lost than I am now. "In truth," he groaned out loud, "it is as though I am already dead." So saying he made the sign of the cross and murmured, "Lord, I who am already dead, I deliver myself unto thee."

"Boy!"

Oswin started up from his sleep in surprise. Father Godwin's face, illuminated by a candle, filled his vision.

"I have brought thee good news, boy!" the monk cried. "My numbers, boy, were in error. Too many naughts. Not enough sixes. And if you take into account certain retrograde stars such as . . ." He waved his hands at Oswin's look of bewilderment. "The point is, boy, the world is *not* yet coming to an end."

"Not at all?" Oswin asked with amazement.

"Nay, not for a while. Thou art safe for the time."

Oswin felt a rush of disappointment. "But . . . Father," he stammered, "if what you say is true . . . I . . . I cannot stay here anymore. Saving thee, there is no one caring for me. The egg that I tried . . ."

"Never mind the egg now. I too have time."

Oswin stared at the monk. "Father, doth thee not hear me? If . . . if I am to live . . . I must flee."

"Ah, good boy, I'm glad thee has come to that. In truth, I will miss thee. For thou art the only one who listens to me. But, God's grace, thee will surely perish if thee stays. Where will thee go?"

"Thee spoke of a village. London . . ."

"Well thought, boy. I think you need only travel due east till thee reach a great river. The Thames, I've heard it called. Follow it. Maybe four, five days journey in all. I'll give you my blessing so you'll come to no harm."

"What will it be like?"

"I cannot say. I've never beheld it. But from what I have heard it cannot, God willing, be worse than thy life here. Indeed, they say there is more food to be found there than in all Christendom. But sleep first. It's very bitter now. Go just before first light."

"Will I truly wake?"

"I promise, thee will wake. Come, let me give thee my blessing." Father Godwin lifted his hand and made the sign of the cross over the boy. Then he bent over and pressed a kiss on Oswin's brow. It was the first kiss the boy ever knew.

As Oswin watched the monk go into the night he suddenly jumped up and called, "Father!"

"Yes, my boy."

"But when *will* the world come to an end and all those things—the dragons, the horsemen, the eagles—that thee said would happen? When will they come?"

"Ah, fear not. I had thought it would in the Year of Our Lord, 1000. But those dreadful things will not pass until the Year of Our Lord, *2000.*"

"And Father," Oswin shouted after him, "will I be alive then?"

"Methinks not. But others will. Thee and I, we will pray for them. God speed thee, boy."

Before dawn, Oswin was on his way. Two hours after he had begun, a golden glow appeared upon the eastern sky. The boy dropped to his knees and began to pray.

Then Oswin looked up. The new day had arrived. He was alive. The prophecy had come true. He had been given life after a living death.

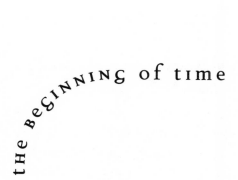

tHe BeGINNING of tIme

■ JaNet tayLoR LisLe

"One thing you need to know is, back in those days, human sacrifice was a big deal," Shelley's nineteen-year-old brother starts off by informing her on the road to Xochicalco that morning. "People were cut open while they were still alive, and their hearts were pulled out for an offering to the gods."

"An early form of organ transplant," Shelley's seventeen-year-old brother, Roddy, assures her with a grin. "They also perfected brain and stomach transplants, and eye and liver transplants, not to mention . . ."

"That will do," Shelley's mother sings out from the front seat. "We all get the idea."

"It's not funny, Rod," James says. "Ancient Mexicans thought time would stop if they didn't give the gods what they wanted. They thought the sun would go out and everything on earth would freeze. In the digs around these places, people keep finding old skeletons with the bones of their chests smashed in. I read about it in *National Geographic* . . . Are you okay, Shell?" he asks. "You look kind of sick."

Immediately, everyone in the family turns and stares at her. Even her father looks via the rearview mirror.

Shelley says she's fine. Hot and squashed, that's all. Who wouldn't be?

All three Morton children are packed into the back seat of a rental car that is proceeding cautiously along a Mexican highway. Outside, the December sun blazes down on brown, parched fields. Gangs of crows patrol the ditches and telephone wires, and Shelley spots the grisly remains of something—a horse?—lying at the side of the road. You saw things like that all the time in Mexico. Animals died along the road and no one bothered to pick them up. They'd just lie there being eaten by birds or ants until nothing was left but a few white bones in the dirt.

The Morton's car, an economy compact, has no air conditioning or radio. Up front, Shelley's father is driving with

both hands gripped on the steering wheel while her mother
tries to read the map. They are going to see an ancient Indian ruin that somebody at the hotel said was good. It's off
in the hills somewhere, they aren't sure where.

"I just realized this map is all in Spanish," Shelley's
mother says. "How am I supposed to read it if it's all in
Spanish?"

"The same way as any other map," her father answers.
"A town is a town. A road is a road. We want the road to
Xochicalco. Do you see Xochicalco?"

Shelley's mother snorts, as if this is the most ridiculous
question she's ever heard. "We're going to get lost," she
says. "I already know it without even looking." She turns
around to Shelley and asks:

"Did you bring your hat? Well, you'll be sorry. It's going
to broil up there on the mountain."

"The thing is," James continues in the patronizing voice
he uses these days to instruct Shelley on what she doesn't
know about the world, which in his view is everything,
"the thing is, there were all these superstitions and laws
that sound totally insane to us now, but back then were like
science. People believed in them.

"Like you had to bury the dead with their feet pointed
west or they wouldn't get into the next world. Or you had
to watch the morning star, who was really the god Quetzalcoatl, for certain signs before you planted the corn.
There was a calendar made up of fifty-two year cycles.

Every fifty-two years was like a century to the ancient Mexicans. Then time would start over again."

"They had a short attention span. Ritalin hadn't been discovered yet," Roddy says, deadpan.

James allows an offended silence to fall after this, as if someone had let loose a bad smell. Then he resumes, patiently, to Shelley.

"They had this story about how time began on earth. Two big, powerful gods—Quetzalcoatl and another guy—saw a beautiful goddess walking along and decided to create the earth from her.

"So they turned themselves into serpents and attacked her from either side. One grabbed her right hand and left foot and the other grabbed her left hand and right foot and they tore her apart. From her parts they made the things of earth.

"Her hair became trees, flowers, and grass. Her cheeks turned into valleys. Her shoulders became mountains. She had started crying, so they made her eyes into little caves with brooks spouting out, and her mouth into big caves and rivers, and all this water flowed down and made oceans, and time on earth began. Pretty amazing, right?"

Shelley looks out the window again. She can't stand being talked to this way. She can't stand being stuck between her brothers, can't stand being reminded of her hat, can't stand Mexico if anyone wants to know—which they don't. They never ask her opinion. She hates the heat, the dirt; even the water is undrinkable. She wishes she could have stayed home to celebrate, like everyone else. But her father had wanted to go somewhere.

"It's the twenty-first century, the millennium, for God's sake!" he'd cried. "We should do something we'll remember. As a family. Go up on some mountain peak and beat our chests."

When she'd looked at her mother's face, Shelley had seen that she didn't want to go anywhere either, but wasn't saying so. That was what her mother always did. She'd go along with whatever Shelley's father wanted to keep the peace. Then, if anything went wrong, she'd say, "I knew it. I had a feeling this would happen."

There is a hierarchy in the Morton family, a sort of pyramid of power shaped not unlike the Indian monuments they've been visiting at Teotihuacan and elsewhere that week. At least, Shelley thinks of it that way.

At the top of the pyramid sits the gray-haired bulk of Grant Morton, her father, insurance executive, college football star in his day, a time that seems, even to him, a few hundred years back now. He still has surges of energy when he'll bellow about chest beating or whatever, but the next thing you know he'll be asleep on the couch in the middle of the Monday night game.

On a lower level, scanning the horizon worriedly for approaching disaster, is Shelley's mother, an intelligent woman and not a bad person if she would just come out and say what she really thinks. Maybe, from keeping the peace all the time, she doesn't know what she thinks anymore. That's the way it looks, sometimes, but Shelley isn't fooled. She thinks her mother knows, she's just hiding out for some reason.

Naturally, from their ledge beneath, James and Roddy take advantage of this. Before long, they're going to be up there on their mother's ledge, and then above it, ordering her around if she doesn't watch out.

James, tall like his father but less athletic, is one of the world's hard-working, serious people. He's majoring in history at college, and is on the debating team, where he tends to lose his cool in close competition and start yelling.

Roddy is smaller, quieter, with a clever sense of humor. You'd never know it from being around him, but come spring he'll graduate number one in his high school class— the class of '00, that is; 2000 A.D.—the year the Morton family is about to cross over into, that very night in fact, the date of this expedition being none other than December 31, 1999.

"I never thought I'd live to see this day," Shelley's mother has already exclaimed twice that morning, though she is only fifty-one and will live on for years more— jogging, avoiding red meat, taking Vitamin E, eating yogurt. Warning Shelley to do the same.

Shelley can't stand yogurt, even the fruit kind.

At the very bottom of the pyramid, in Mexico or wherever they happen to be, is Shelley.

Little Shell.

Her family still calls her that, a name left over from toddlerhood. For one thing, though now fourteen, she still *is* little, as light and fine-boned as one of the marsh birds that saunter around the Morton's shoreline home in Connecticut. Her hips are as narrow as a ten-year-old boy's and her T-shirts lie flat against her chest. Nothing, it seems, is going to get her body going into grown-upness, into flesh and curves and the correct appearance of the normal human female.

"Late bloomer" people call girls like her, and like many late bloomers she is shy, reserved. Of course, she has been carefully brought up, too, not to be the sort of girl who goes looking for help from lipstick or high-heeled boots, push-up bras, or eyelash curlers.

She will have to wait, that's all; wait for nature to catch her up and pull her along, though she does get a little impatient sometimes. She's begun to wonder lately: Is there something she's doing that's holding her back while other girls her age are surging ahead? Some set of mind. Some fear of . . . what?

She doesn't know.

She braids her long, thin, pale hair down her back in a single plait, the way she's always worn it. Her mother likes it that way, though it makes Shelley look even younger than she is, more innocent, vulnerable before life's darker truths, it's evils, of which she's supposedly ignorant (well, admit it, she probably is ignorant) and from which she has been carefully protected since birth, being the baby and the only girl. Her whole family is dedicated to this proposition: Keep little Shell safe!

"You stay close when we get there," Shelley's mother turns around to say to her in the car. "No wandering off on your own this time. I could have killed you at Puebla."

"Oh Mother, I only went to the bathroom!"

"Well, tell me next time. We're in a foreign country. Bathrooms aren't always safe."

"Mother, give me a break!"

They turn off the highway.

Shelley sees a dead dog lying in a ditch, eyes thick with flies, a gray tongue lolled out the side of its jaw. The road goes through a dusty, exhausted-looking town where chickens peck the dirt and laundry hangs in trashy front yards. A ragged man with a crutch crosses slowly in front of them.

"Is this the right way?" her father asks.

"How should I know?" her mother answers. She reaches back and lifts her shoulder-length hair off her neck so the clasp of her gold necklace shows, then lets the hair fall irritably.

"I'll look. Where's the map?" James says. Roddy leans over to examine it, too.

"Get off! You're suffocating me," Shelley tells him, shoving him away. Her chest feels tight, as if it wants to explode.

They begin to go uphill on a narrow, asphalt road. Then they are in the woods, weaving up and up through a series of hairpin turns with no place to turn around even if they wanted to. The trees are too close on either side, too tangled together. The sun is invisible and the light filtering through has a gray-green cast, like mold. A new sense is born in the minds of the travelers that they have crossed some divide, have embarked on a venture in which retreat, or even a prudent change of plans, are no longer options.

The words "forest primeval" come into Shelley's head and she can't get them out. A droning chant starts inside her, in time to the motor's throb.

Forest Primeval! Forest Primeval!

The more she chants, the darker and more exhillarating the forest around her seems to grow. She almost begins to wish they would get lost, or that the car would break down, so she could leap away like a wild deer and run out into it.

Not that she would really do that, of course. It's just a crazy thought that comes into her head.

They go down into a mean little valley, pass by shacks, fields of rubbish and broken-down farm machinery. Then

up again into utter wilderness, the car engine laboring nois-
ily, now hiccuping when they have to slow down at the
curves. In the middle of one curve, it stalls out completely
and Shelley's father has to stop and put on the hand brake
before starting the car again because the incline is so steep.

"Altitude," he snaps at James to cover up his nerves.
"What do you guess we're at?"

"I'd say eight, maybe ten thousand feet," James replies.
"How's your gas?"

"About a third of a tank. I think I should've filled her
up before we set off," Shelley's father more or less bellows.

After another minute, though, the road widens and lev-
els out, and they seem to be getting somewhere.

They pass a group of country Mexicans walking along
the roadside. They're carrying sacks and look as if they
might have been picking something under the trees. Or
looking for something to pick. Their faces turn as the Morton's car comes up and follow it as it goes by. One woman
is carrying a pouch on her back that is tied crosswise. Her
baby?

Shelley has seen women carrying babies this way in the
markets they've visited. The people in Mexico are much
smaller than in America. Shelley has seen women who
were as small as children, children as tiny as dolls. It
shocked her.

She's walked past a figure she assumed from the back

was a little girl of seven or eight, and then seen her face and realized she was a woman. A mother, even, with a child.

"It's because they don't get enough protein," Shelley's mother had said. "For generations, not enough food."

But Shelley had seen other small women in the town squares, wearing tight pants, spike heels and mascara, and when she looked in their faces, she saw they were no older than she was.

The Mortons have traveled for over an hour in the shadowy, forested mountains without seeing anyone. They've begun to believe again that they are lost. A number of angry accusations about this have been made, and a tense silence has settled over the car, when the forest suddenly falls away and they are there.

Xochicalco. High up on the side of a mountain. Clear air. Sun. A tremendous view of the surrounding country. They pull into a flat dirt area that seems to be for parking and see they are almost the first ones. Two other cars in the whole lot.

"Now who says we shouldn't have come!" Shelley's father exults. "Look at this place! Look!"

"The fearless explorers emerge from the dark heart of the jungle, miracle of all miracles," Roddy drawls. "So, Dad, should we beat our chests now or later?"

Shelly bursts out laughing and everyone else does, too, from relief more than anything. For a few seconds, she feels the day inflate with joy: they are all smiling at each other, all in balance, one happy family traveling in the same direction.

They get out of the car and immediately Shelley's mother ruins things by looking pointedly at her and saying, "Anyone for the restroom before we start?"

Shelley gets so angry—which is not a way she normally gets—that she walks off without waiting for the others. For some reason, another time when she was eight years old comes into her mind and she remembers how mad she got when her piano teacher, Mr. Hazarian, was sent away.

No one would explain the reason why. Her parents tried to tell her some lies about how he was only teaching older children now, how he was too busy for her. She knew that couldn't be true because she and Mr. Hazarian had been friends. They'd really liked each other. He appreciated her serious attitude, spoke to her kindly and respectfully about her playing.

Later, her mother had cleared up the mystery by saying:

"He sat too close to you on the bench. I didn't like it, the way he sat. And we'd heard some things."

"What things?"

"He'd had some trouble with other students. We had to let him go."

Shelley never asked any more about it. She knew her

mother didn't want her to ask so she kept quiet, but inside, she was angry.

James catches up with her and they walk around the ruins together. From a guide book, he reads to her about what various things are.

Wide stone steps go up onto a vast grassy terrace that was once the sacred dwelling of high priests and their astronomers. Some big stone slabs and pillars with carvings on them, of birds and snakes, people and corn, are a record of happenings in the far past.

At one time over a thousand years ago, Xochicalco had been a meeting place for ancient Mexican cultures. Great leaders had come there to iron out the problem of time. The trouble was that each culture was using a different method to calculate it. Days were shorter or longer, months were fewer or more numerous, years and centuries were completely different lengths depending on which group you came from. There was no universal history because no one could agree when anything had happened.

"Did they finally agree on something?" Shelley asks, trailing along behind James.

"They agreed on fifty-two-year centuries, remember?" James says. "Until the Spanish Conquistadors came and took over. They changed everything to our time, four weeks, twelve months, three hundred and sixty-five days. It's not perfect but it works."

"Could anything be better?" Shelley asks.

"I don't see how," James replies.

Across the terrace, Shelley sees a flash of movement. They have been followed. A small gang of men in muscle shirts and Levis has slipped quietly up the steps she and James have just come up. They veer off and turn their backs when they see they're being watched, and pretend to gaze over the wall.

"James, look."

There are six. They are not tourists. They're lean and dangerous-looking, with dark, handsome faces and evasive eyes. One has something in his hand that might be a knife. He tosses it in the air, catches it, tosses it up again. The others glance slyly over their shoulders.

"He's got a switchblade," James whispers.

"What should we do?"

"Move slow. Act like nothing's wrong. There's a staircase over there. We're going to walk toward it."

They walk, feeling as if they're moving underwater. When they get to the stairway, they can't stop themselves from running. Shelley takes the steps two at a time.

"Where are Mother and Dad?" James pants beside her. "We haven't seen them for a while."

"I don't know."

"We should go look for them."

They come out on another grass terrace, turn right and run around some big stones, then head down again.

"Somewhere around here is the ball court," James says. "Dad wanted to see that. They might be there." He stops and rifles through the guide book for the map they were following before. Shelley's heart is thudding against her ribs.

"Could it be down there?" she asks, pointing.

They ignore the winding tourist path and run directly down a sloping hillside. The ball court is at the bottom, a long, narrow, grass playing field running between vertical walls of stone. On top of the walls are rows of stone seats from which a fair-size audience might look down on the action. Shelley and James crouch down between some seats, and look back up the hill.

"I think we lost them," James says.

"Were they really trying to get us?" Shelley asks in amazement.

"We didn't want to hang around and find out."

"What should we do now?"

"Stay here. Dad was coming here, I know. We'll never find them if we keep moving," James says.

He opens the guide book and reads to Shelley, a little shakily, about the ball court.

An ancient kind of football was played on the court. The players, who competed in teams but also separately, could score by passing the ball through a heavy stone ring attached sideways to the wall at midcourt. It was a test of speed and skill, but ended, strangely enough, in violence. The game's high scorer was rewarded by being put to death before the crowd.

"The winner was killed? But why?" Shelley asks.

"It was another form of sacrifice. They were beaten to death," James says, glancing up toward the terraces again. The absurdity of this cruel end gives Shelley a little jolt.

"Not a nice place," she comments, though it's actually rather pretty there. The grass is as lush as green velvet and birds zip eagerly from one perch to another around the court. The silence between the walls is so deep that their bird voices ring out distinctly on the air, a never-ending medley of chirps and raucous cries.

"I still don't see Mother and Dad," James says. "Or Roddy."

The toughs seem not to have followed them. After the drama of their flight, Shelley feels a bit let down.

"Mother will find us. She always does," she says. "We can't stay here all day."

"I guess we could go see the caves," James answers. "Maybe they'll be there."

"What caves?"

"There are ancient caves under the hillside. Come on, I'll show you."

The sun is now directly overhead, nearly blinding them with its brightness. The day is heating up and Shelley thinks of the hat she left behind, then realizes she will soon be undercover so it doesn't matter. They go down another level to a row of subterranean entrances that lead back into the cool earth.

" 'The Eye of God'," James reads out from the guide book. "That's the cave we want. 'A single, piercing beam of light descends into the cave through a fissure high in the stone ceiling above. At certain hours, depending on the season, this beam achieves an X-ray intensity that can penetrate skin to illuminate the bones inside. A place of religious and mystical power in early Toltec culture.' "

"Sounds interesting. Where is it?" Shelley asks.

They go into one cave, then another, and then, with a third try, seem to have found what they are looking for, because way at the end of a dark tunnel they see a bright light shafting down. They are about to go inside when . . .

"Halloo! Halloo!" Shelley hears her mother's voice in the distance. "Wait! Wait for us!"

"There they are," James says, turning around with relief.

Far across and up on an opposite stone stairway, the figures of the three lost Mortons materialize. Roddy is sitting on one of the steps, his head propped thoughtfully between his hands. Shelley's parents are both waving frantically, and already walking in their direction.

"See? No need to worry," James says. "They'll be here in a minute."

"I wasn't worrying," Shelley says. "I was trying to get away."

Instantly, it seems to be true. Her irritation at her mother flares up again. She desires nothing more than to remove herself from her mother's line of vision, to step away from the insidious grasp of this family that is always around her, keeping her small and helpless, smothered—yes, smothered, literally!—so she can hardly breathe anymore. The blazing heat of Mexico has just made it worse. She is boxed in everywhere, wherever she goes, in cars, in rooms, in her own clothes and body.

James has begun to walk off toward the rest of the family. He swings across the grass on his long legs. Roddy is on his feet, bounding down the steps. They will meet in the middle, where decisions will be made.

They will go for lunch. They will head for the restrooms. They will get undercover, the sun is too bright now. They will go up onto the high terraces again or they will not. Decisions will be made and Shelley will have no part in them, as usual. Her condition will be noted, as a child's is: She is sunburned, she is hungry, she is grumpy and needs rest. But her real person will not be consulted, will never be consulted, not for years and years to come. This is the dreadful future that suddenly spreads out in front of her, an absolute horror of a future.

When James has gone a good distance away and her

parents are still far across the grass, Shelley does something she didn't expect to do. She ducks into the Eye of God cave and begins to walk down the long tunnel.

No sooner is she inside than she realizes that others are there ahead of her. A thunder of voices is echoing down the walls. She hears the dangerous rasp of male laughter. By then, though, nothing in the world could have dragged her back and she just keeps walking.

The sound of Shelley's footsteps echo ahead of her down the tunnel and by the time she comes to the round cave room at the end, the laughing and voices have fallen silent. She stands in the narrow tunnel opening and sees their six shapes around the wall—the bright light pouring down in the center puts all else in shadow—and recognizes them. It's the gang from the high terrace. She can't see their faces or which one is the one with the knife, but their menacing slouches are unmistakable.

She feels an impulse to look back to see if James or any of her family is there, but resists it. Any show of doubt or fear will work against her. Besides, she would know without looking if anyone came because sound travels so perfectly in this place. Every rustle and breath is audible. She hears the men in front of her, shifting their weight, taking their hands out of their pockets, even turning their heads—

the barely perceptible hiss their necks make against the sides of their collars.

She hadn't known a tiny motion like a turned neck could make such a frightening noise.

Well, she can't stand there forever. She puts her hands on her narrow hips and steps forward toward the center of the cave where the shaft of light falls. Along the wall, the bodies also shift position, move around her, keeping their backs to the stone, as if a slow game were beginning.

Her father would speak now, she thinks. He would use his voice to dominate the scene and bring it under his control. So would James, and perhaps even Roddy and her mother would try. But Shelley knows she must not speak. Her voice is still a girl's voice and they would only laugh. They would see how young she was, how power-less, beneath the dignity of their sport, the way a child would be.

No, she will not take refuge there anymore. Never again, whatever happens. She will say nothing, will keep her hands on her hips, cool, brazen, like the girls in the Puebla market. She thrusts her chin up and goes forward again, feeling a little lightheaded but stepping surely into the eye, the beam of light pouring down from the ceiling.

When she is directly under it, she raises her hands to it and, it's true! Her bones are revealed. Through her skin, she sees her finger bones, her arm bones, the sinewy connection of her wrist bones, and for the first time she understands herself to be a creature made of bone. Not only flesh, but hard bone. She puts her hands back on her hips and stares up into the light.

Eye of God, she thinks. Tell me what to do next, you Eye of God.

She is aware that the men are moving again, rearranging themselves in some way she can't see. The cave is not that big, maybe fifteen feet across, but she's inside the light now, and can't make out even their shapes. Blackness surrounds her. She hears a loud click, the sound of a heel dislodging a pebble. Except that's not what it is. She knows: it's the flick of the switchblade coming open.

She had expected them to stop her before now. She expects it this instant and at every instant, now and now, her nerves stretched almost beyond endurance. But they continue to circle her without touching or speaking. Their shoes' rustling against the stone floor is like the slide of serpents.

Another click rings out and she turns toward it, fiercely, to show that she is not afraid. Then, with the hot beam pouring down on her head, she's surprised by a sudden inspiration. Reaching behind her back, she brings her long braid forward over one shoulder, pulls off the elastic band and begins slowly to undo the strands.

Not once does she look down at the work her fingers

do. She stares straight into the darkness to hold the shapes still, to keep them off a bit longer with the slow dance of her hands.

Silence falls and a miracle begins to happen. She feels their eyes on her and knows that she has begun to charm them, to confuse them. They meant to hurt her but now cannot. She is fascinating to them as a woman is fascinating to men, as a power, a light, a flesh-and-bone stranger. A woman. Not a breath comes out of them, not a foot moves, and for the space of this miracle, which may be centuries or seconds by the ordinary measure, time stops everywhere on earth. It just stops.

When, after an eternity, Shelley finishes unbraiding her hair, she runs her fingers up through it and spreads it in a sparkling tent all over her shoulders. She remains still for a moment to test the strength of her spell. Then she turns and steps out of the light and walks away free as air down the long tunnel. And time starts up. It begins all over again.

Years later, when Shelley told this story to people—to friends and passing acquaintances, to her children and, even later, to her grandchildren—she would always call it her "Eye of God" story. Because she must have been saved by the grace of God, she would say, or maybe by the grace of *the gods,* since it seemed likely that older, more primitive, powers were in charge in that cave.

Not that gods always step in like that, you understand, she would say. They're unpredictable, at best, even in their own caves. Gods like a bit of sport as well as anyone. In fact, ninety-nine out of a hundred people in a situation like hers would have come out hurt, if they came out at all. I was lucky, she'd say. The truth is, those gods were probably all out to lunch that day. They'll catch up with me some day, then I'll be sorry.

Shelley could be quite funny on this subject of gods and the vaguaries of fate. It turned out that some of her brother Roddy's knack for humor had rubbed off on her. Or perhaps it was a passing of the mantle since, impossible as it was for her to believe then, or even years afterwards, Roddy, their wonderful, funny, brilliant Roddy, had been killed in a boat accident only six months after this trip to Mexico.

Shelley's parents had never really recovered from the shock. They had lived on, quietly, in the shadow of a cruelty they could not even talk about, much less comprehend. And Shelley had lived on, too, of course. She grew up, put on weight, graduated from college. She married and had three children, two daughters with her first husband and, after a sad and drawn-out divorce, a son with her second husband.

She'd held three jobs, been fired twice, quit the last and gone into business for herself as a landscape designer. She'd been in a bad car crash and nearly lost a leg, but was rewarded when a woman she met at the rehab clinic became an irreplacable friend for life.

Thereafter, she walked with a limp and oh, a thousand other things happened. Her son was mugged. Her husband was promoted. Their house caught on fire. She got the contract she wanted. Her business failed. Her daughter had twins. She saw the Great Wall of China. Her father died. She grew closer to her mother.

Her life fanned out behind her like the vast train of a ballgown, picking up debris, dropping it, sweeping all before it, leaving much in its wake, snagging on things, wrenching loose, tearing, getting mended, wearing thin, sailing along anyway, trailing back for miles and miles behind her, dragging her down but also steadying her, holding her up as she walked, as she kept walking, forward.

The question Shelley was inevitably asked when she had finished telling her Eye of God story was why she kept going down that tunnel when she knew the dangerous gang was there. She'd heard them in plenty of time to stop. Why hadn't she turned around? Why couldn't she have found another, safer cave, if she had to get away from her family so badly?

Shelley would always laugh and say, "But I had to go. There was no choice. I could no more have turned back than I could have stopped living and turned into stone."

Then someone would always ask if her parents had been angry when she came out and found them.

They weren't. Everyone thought she had gone to the bathroom again. In fact, she never even told them what had happened in the cave because she didn't want to frighten them. Think how they would have worried!

Someone else would want to know if they all made it back to the hotel that day.

Yes, they had, she'd say. That little rented car got amazing gas mileage. Or maybe the gas meter was broken, because they still had a quarter of a tank when they got back to town.

What she didn't bother to go on and tell was this:

That evening, the Morton family went up on the roof of the hotel after dinner to watch fireworks in honor of the millennium, and then to wait for the clock to tick down.

Finally it did, and a thousand years rolled over into the past, and a new thousand-year cycle started up without a whimper. There was not one flash from the stars, the great volcano at Mt. Popo didn't explode, the earth didn't open up and swallow anybody.

Roddy and James, who later went on to teach history and have a family himself, and Shelley's parents, for whom this trip would be the last with all their children, went to bed feeling disappointed that the passage hadn't been more extraordinary.

But Shelley lay in her bed with a great, black cave inside her, and the certainty that she had been seen as she would be. And she was right, she had been seen. The future was coming for her as fast and furiously as the two serpent gods in James' story.

cLay

■ RITa wILLIamS-garcIa

L ay down that Spoon. It's time to go. Time
to go."
    "Ain't quite done stirrin."
"Past time. Lay it down."
"One more turn. Keep it going, keep it going."
"Can't do no more than we done. Lay it down,
Old Wife. Time to go."

Homecoming used to mean canning, quilting,
storytelling. Opening our arms to loved ones
home from city living. Now as we stand on the

stoop of the New Day, homecoming is slipping away. Especially from us mothers watching the world whirl through our small town. We note it's odd markings on Six Mules and how we're the only ones resisting the pull. Stirring against it. Beating it into the clay.

Wsss . . . the world spins on, stealing grain beneath our feet. *Wsss.* Faster than arms can gather and root. All we can do is steady our clay pots, raise wooden spoons, then stir.

> *Ca lunk lunk clak*
> *Ca lunk lunk clak*
> *Keep it going, keep it going.*
> *Ca lunk lunk clak*
> *Ca lunk lunk clak*
> *Stir against the world.*

When we draw an even pull between the earth's spinning and our stirring, we lay down our spoons, at least for the time being, though lately it gets harder and harder for me to rest. A feeling comes over me, something unsettling, like sitting on an outbound train knowing I've left rice simmering on the stove. This is how us Town Mothers are about the New Day. No matter how much we stir and prepare for it, there's that feeling that something's left undone.

Further back than any one of us can recall, homecoming simply was. Folks sent their restless young out into the

world, then welcomed them back—as long as they didn't
track in too much dirt.

Now homecoming is set aside for the New Day Celebration. Now it's a big fuss here, panic there. Herding folks
into seminars over things that can easily get fixed with a
flex of common sense. Passing the hat to pay celebrity guest
speakers from the outside who wouldn't know Six Mules to
squat on it.

Gone is the simple need to shake off the world and be
among the familiar. Those of us old enough to remember
are seldom asked to Tell. Lately, those who are called upon
to Tell the stories of Six Mules lop off the limbs and heart.
And now, there's no room for the Telling in the New Day
celebration program. All of this hoopla over the passing of
years. None of it won't mean a thing if there's no home to
to come back to.

At the New Day Celebration Empowerment Seminar, (this
used to be the homecoming sewing circle) the Six Mules
Ladies Club presented us—Myrt, Thel, Lilla Mae, and
me—with an award for being "Exemplary Mothers." This
they did as a mockery to our having nine, ten, eleven, and
fourteen kids. It was as if The Ladies Club said "They
didn't become doctors, moneymakers, and muckety-mucks
but they birthed a few. Let's give them an award that they
don't look useless."

We shake our heads, accept our award, and wait for the poetry recital, only to learn there will be none.

"No recital? No recital?"

"No, Mama," my oldest girl says in that shush tone. "Poetry recitals and storytelling are homecoming events. This is a whole new day."

How could this be? More than a century ago we crossed the Mississippi with our work songs. Over decades the work song churned into the blues verse, and verse into poems. Angry poems to stir the soul. *Umh.* I see cutting up bits of *Cane*—our favorite reader from back in the day—and grinding it into clay pots didn't exactly grow us no poets.

Instead of the poetry recital we sat through a host of preachers, politicians, and the (heh, heh) "learned" jockeying for their place in the New Day. Instead of worrying how we'll spell their names, they ought to think about what's simmering on the stove. What's gonna get left back while we're all marching forward. They just ought to give a listen to what we Town Mothers know about Six Mules.

It was our mothers' mothers that seen the town come out of six "just freed" families, pulling six mules through 240 acres. Those are some women can Tell it, and if we'd listen we'd know we came from strong stuff and our children would lead us into the New Day and beyond.

Our own mothers never pulled no plow, but they

walked the land in bare feet, turning the soil black and rich for growing, particularly mushrooms. The kind of mushrooms restaurants far as St. Louis and 'Frisco crave for wine cooking. From mushrooms alone money poured in. Commerce germed, starting with a store, a beauty parlor, a bait shop, and a school.

But it was our eyes that seen Six Mules step out from under dried blood of the hanging pine. It was gals like myself, Myrt, Thel, and Lilla Mae could see the backdoor swing shut on one century, and the next door far off, but open for us to walk through. We had our hopes on a dream. A revolutionary dream.

Being that we were the new generation of women having babies in hospitals, we read everything, but listened carefully to what our mothers said about hospital birthings. Yet and so, wasn't 'a one of us who didn't secretly feel the glamour of a hospital birth. We couldn't keep still from giggling as our mothers explained: " 'Bove all, don't let 'em tape no quarter to that baby's belly to shape the navel. Get that stump tied so it can fall off at home." Got so that when the nurse saw a Six Mules woman coming in they told the doctors, "No quarter on that one. Just tie the stump. Don't ask why. It's religious or something."

We did as our mothers showed us. (The basic thing we all knew from having sisters and brothers underfoot.) It was the intimate details of motherhood that excited us. The secrets Mama let us in on because we were now one:

"Clip the first growth of hair. Get a lock tight and curly. Nain't while be too quick to 'merse the baby in water. Let baby's natural earth mix with the soil that the house sits on. Scrap his earthy dirt from the folds of his skin, inside his ear and such. Get a clay jar from the In'ian compound. Clay, y'hear? And a plain wooden mixing spoon. When the stump fall off wrap it in 'lyptus leaves for keepin' and let it set in the earth in the pot. Whatever you do, keep a watch over what goes in, y'hear? Keep it going, keep it going. The rest will come as motherin' sets in."

> *Ca lunk lunk clak*
> *Ca lunk lunk clak*
> *Keep it going, keep it going*

Every mother had one. A sound made while mixing the child's ingredients into the clay pot. Each child's coming brought something new to the clay.

Clak lak a-lak lak, high on the edge. *Low low b low low,* down at the base. *Shhhr shhrr shhhrr,* blend it sun and moon. Keep it going, keep it going.

Whatever mother thought was needed for the child to grow right went into the pot. Poetry, stolen shavings from Doc's 'scription pad, wild yam root, cardomon seeds, road tar. Every mother had her eye on a revolutionary dream, stirring it, watching it, growing it, like our mothers done for us.

I does mine on the hip. Myrt holds hers on her lap. Thel,

'gainst the breastbone. Lilla Mae leans it sideways like it's gonna spill, but she got it going, just a-going.

With every mother beatin' the clay pot and watching the ingredients that stirred into every child, wasn't a whole lot to worry about, which made Six Mules a fine place for raising kids. Every child was watched, every child thought of. Was no such thing as worrying about this one's child was the bully, that one's child had a knife, this one's child kept that one from learning, 'cause every child's mama had a clay pot, and kept count of what went into each child. So even if there was a slack mama, only halfway watching her pot, the rest of us mamas kept a watch for her.

Our own mothers frowned on what we threw in the clay pots. They had called us modern women, stirring more poetry and road tar than wild yam root and earth, as they had done. Yet and still, Big Daughter laughed at me, because, as she put it, "TV mothers don't beat clay pots." When she thought my back was turned I caught her reciting a poem to her sisters and brothers that started, "Your mama stir voodoo, out of greasy grits and doodoo."

"Let 'em laugh," I told Myrt, Lilla Mae, and Thel. "Least they know not to touch our clay pots."

On that, we could trust our training. We never kept anything from our kids' reach. If anything, they had good sense.

Then come itchy, fishy smelling first love, and showing Big Daughter what her body was in relation to the earth and Son. "Oh that? We had that sex education stuff in school. We know all that, Mama."

Ca lunk lunk clak. Sometimes it was just nerves. We had to stir.

I recall feeling the gentle pull of Mama's hand easing the spoon from my fist as I stirred my clay pot. It was the night before Big Daughter's first school dance. Mama said, "N'aint while beat on that so hard. His mama been stirring 'long side you from day one. Best save that navel stump for something real."

Mama was right.

Myrt's oldest was marching in '63. We stirred our clay pots. In '64 the sons of the KKK threw dynamite into Thel's baby's dormitory at med school. We worked stumps from the birth cord. In '66 Lilla Mae's girl slipped through a bungled plot by the feds. We worked stumps and roots and stirred.

But in 1967, Thel, Myrt, Lilla Mae, and I watched four of our Daughters *ca lunk lunk clak* and twenty-three of our Sons *ca lunk lunk clak* went off to Vietnam. We called on stumps, roots, and earth waves that "came from no wheres" according to them seismographin' geniuses at the Institute. Had they been in tuned, theyda known that earthquake bore out of a faithful stir from clay pots, porch to porch from the country's navel. And it shook the world and stopped everything.

For the first and only time, Big Daughter took up the

wooden spoon to keep it going, keep it going / send a wave through the core / run a wave through the ocean / crack the earth's skull / from raw birth rope / bring the earth to the Sons and the Sons to their earth / keep it going, keep it going.

I didn't lay down my spoon until 1968, when eighteen came home whole. Six came home whole in '69. But in 1970 the last two came home carrying their brother's dog tags to give to Thel.

Having some pity on our failure, my oldest son said it was for the best. Said not to tell Thel, but the Son that left wouldn't have been the one to come back. I said, "We could have stirred—" and he said, "Not against heroin."

I just couldn't imagine what a child could be, that a mother couldn't have them in her home.

Son just said, "Mama, there are things in this world . . . things in this world. . . ."

Since that time, Big Daughter went north for an education, married a son from up there. A son weaned from a concrete tit, and no clay pot stirred in his name.

I started to pack for a visit with the news of the first Grand. My kids, from the oldest down to the baby, set out to teach me about the city, as though I new nothing of the world I stirred against. They went so far as to tell me how to read faces. How to fold money. How to walk. What to do with my smile on a crowded boulevard. Mama chuckled.

Not ten feet from the Greyhound stop, I saw they were

right. Sons jumping Grannys for pocketbooks. Fathers wifing down their Daughters. Gals emptying Babies with the trash. Everything but an ounce of kindness spilling from mamas' mouths.

My new Son welcomed me into their home.

I put a bonafide clay pot and a wooden spoon on the kitchen counter. With some dirt from home, I planted a vine.

"Lookin' at you," I told Daughter. "I see you won't stir this clay pot. All I ask is that you watch the vine. Keep it growing."

As Daughter and her husband slept I put my Grand's earth in the clay pot and hoped for roots. A Grandma does what she can.

Then I came home.

Big Daughter wasn't the only child with road tar stuck to her heels. Seven of mine had gone out beyond Six Mules to have wives, husbands, and children. Eight of Thel's went. Nine of Myrt's. All of Lilla Mae's.

Even the ones that stayed seemed to have gone—or have wandered far off, with their eyes on the New Day. Not how we saw it for them, but how they saw it for themselves.

We shake our heads.

The first day of the New Day Celebration was all we could stand. Thel, Myrt, Lilla Mae, and I retreated to our homes and waited for the commotion and panic to die

CLAY

down and for common sense to return. After all, it's not the passing of time that needs celebrating, but what you do with it.

For all of our stirring and shaping our kids' ways, we are just perplexed. Instead of coming together to sew quilts, we piece together our childrens' ways and try to figure where they're heading. (Lilla Mae wonders if we were right to have stirred in road tar.) Mama, who still calls us modern women, chuckles to herself.

Oh, we still make room for our Daughters, Sons, and Grands when they come back to Six Mules, but homecoming has just about died. Even though no one but us Town Mothers will stir in the New Day, we can't help but feel something is left undone. I know it. Myrt and Thel feel it. Lilla Mae says it's sad and true; the world is bigger than our clay pots.

Us Town Mothers will continue to do what Town Mothers do, while the laser shows go on, and the seminars drone on, and speakers speak about everything but Six Mules. But now, when our children and grandchildren come in from their New Day Celebration, we'll put away our clay pots and stirring spoons, someplace high and out of reach.

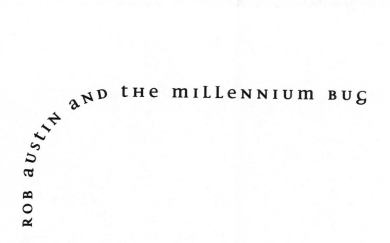

ROB AUSTIN AND THE MILLENNIUM BUG

■ MADELEINE L'ENGLE

It was a snowy Saturday afternoon in early December, not a gentle snow, but a steady descending of great white flowers, so big you could almost see their geometrical patterns. The ground was whitening rapidly. The branches of the trees were outlined in white. Contrary to our usual busy Saturday pattern we were all in the house. John, my elder brother, would usually be out in the barn, which he called his lab, working on some scientific project. John's the eldest and good at science and he tends to be bossy, otherwise he's okay. I, Vicky, come next. I had my journal on my lap along with a paperback copy of *Jane Eyre,* which I was reading for at least the fifth time. Suzy had made a big pot of cocoa. "I'm going to use marshmallows instead of whipped cream. It's quicker, and I'm not sure there's any cream in the fridge."

"Um." I turned a page, paying more attention to Mr. Rochester than the cocoa.

Rob, our little brother, lay under the dining table setting up his wooden trains and making train noises. The house smelled of fragrant smoke from the applewood fire and the tantalizing odor of the roast mother was simmering in the crock pot.

Despite the weather, Mother was not here. Early in the morning before the snow started, she had taken off with a friend to do some major shopping, because the sales were on. We were all at the age where we grew out of our clothes when you turned your back, and John in particular needed some new shirts where the sleeves would come down at least to his wrist bones.

Our father, as usual, was at the hospital, though he was supposed to be through after lunch on Saturdays. Since there are four of us, you couldn't exactly say that we were alone in the house, but at least it was just us kids and not our parents.

Earlier in the day, Suzy and Rob had cut blocks of snow to make a very wobbly igloo, but now, at a little after four, with dark closing in, they had come back into the house and were sitting in front of the fire. John and I had brought in stacks of wood in case the power went out, which it often does when the snow lies heavy on the trees.

Suddenly, Rob jumped up and pointed to the hearth. "Look at that bug!"

"It's just a cricket," John said.

Suzy, the entomologist, peered at the bug and shook her head. "It's not a cricket."

"It's an enormous beetle," Rob pronounced.

"Don't step on it," Suzy warned, looking at John whose foot was raised as though to demolish the bug.

Suzy rushed out to the pantry and came back with two paper cups. Using one as a shovel, she managed to get the bug into the other.

"Now what are you going to do with it?" John asked.

"I rescued it. Now I've got to set it free." Before we could stop her she lifted the big iron latch on the east door. It banged open and large quantities of snow came in. She threw the bug out, cup and all, and then it took all four of us to get the door shut and latched again.

Mother came in from the garage carrying armfuls of packages. "Don't open that door again. I've never felt the wind so strong."

"I hope the bug is okay," Suzy said.

"It's only a bug." John took the packages from Mother and put them on the table.

Rob said, "But maybe it's a millennium bug."

"Honestly, Rob!" Suzy used her most scornful tone. "The millennium bug is not a real bug. It's an imaginary concept to explain all the things that could happen when the century's over."

I looked up from my book and grinned at Suzy. "It's not going to be very imaginary on New Year's Eve when all the power goes out."

At that moment the lights flickered and we were in the semi dark; the room was lit by the fire. There was no comforting hum from the furnace or the fridge. All the usual noises were silenced. When the snow started we had prepared for a possible power outage by filling the bathtub and several large pots with water. The pump to our well is triggered by electricity, so if the power goes out we lose water, too. Lots of places have town or city water, but in our part of the village we all have our own wells.

Rob moved so that he was sitting close to me. "It was my bug. I found it, and Suzy shouldn't have thrown it out."

"I didn't hurt it," Suzy said defensively. "I rescued it."

"You threw it out," Rob said, "and the power went out."

"It had nothing to do with the bug!"

"Keep it to a quiet roar," Mother said. She took three of the big stubby candles we keep for emergencies and lit them. Then she went to the stove, lifted the lid off the crock pot, sniffed, and put the lid back on. "The pot roast is done, and it will just go on cooking in its own juices for hours."

John sniffed appreciatively. "Anything we can do to help?"

"Everything's under control, for the present at least."

Rob said, "Suzy threw out the millennium bug."

Mother said, "That's enough, Rob."

Suzy spoke in a loud voice. "It's only the first week in December. The millennium doesn't happen till December thirty-first turns into January first, and there isn't any millennium bug anyhow."

"You threw it out," Rob reiterated.

John asked, "Rob, do you know what a millennium is?"

"Sure. We had it in school. It's a thousand years."

I shut my book and put it on the floor. "And at the end of this year we'll have finished another thousand years."

"And there may be problems, big problems," Suzy said darkly.

"Why?" I asked. "We got through one thousand, and then another thousand. So why should this one be such a big problem?"

"Computers," John said. "A thousand years ago we didn't have computers."

"So?" I opened *Jane Eyre* again, but I'd more or less lost interest.

Mother said, "It's because we're on the binary system."

"What's that got to do with it?" Suzy asked.

I intoned, quoting the Red Queen from *Through the*

Looking Glass, " 'What's one and one and one and one and one.' That's binary."

"No," John contradicted. "It's one two, one two, one two. So the problem is that we dropped nineteen."

"Nineteen?"

John explained, "The early computers didn't have the big memories they have today, so to save space they dropped nineteen."

"Nineteen what?" I had started to read again. Jane Eyre didn't have any computer problems.

Mother explained, "Nineteen, as in the date. Say someone was born in 1944, and if we say that person was born in '44, they'd understand it was *1*944."

John nodded. "We talk about the music of the forties being revived, and everybody knows we mean 1944, not 1844, or 1344. So when we come to 1999, because we've dropped the nineteen, the computers haven't been programmed to change nineteen to twenty, and they'll drop us right back to 1900, right, Mother?"

She shut the fridge door. "Unless they all get reprogrammed. I can change my watch myself, and a few other things, like the microwave. The problem will be with the big systems, the hospitals, and banks, and the telephone companies. There are a great many engineers working on the big computers, but they might not get them all done in time."

Rob asked, "You mean the computer can't do it by itself?"

John shook his head. "When there's any big change that affects computer systems, it all has to be reprogrammed by human beings."

Suzy said, "So human beings made the mess by leaving out nineteen, and now human beings have to get us out of it."

I looked at the flame on one of the candles. Jane Eyre didn't have electricity. She'd had to use candles.

"It wouldn't be so bad here for us. We're used to having the power go out. But it could be terrible for people in the cities."

Rob stood up and walked away and I could hear the pantry door bang shut in the wind. When he came back he had on his snowsuit and boots.

"Where do you think you're going?" John managed to slam the door shut.

"I'm going to find that bug that Suzy threw out."

"Oh, Rob, don't be silly," Suzy groaned.

Rob looked at her calmly. "If there's a millennium bug out there, I'm going to find it."

"Good for you," Mother said. "Give me a minute to get my things on and I'll go with you."

Who knows? I'm not a scientist like John and Suzy. I know it's a metaphorical and not a real bug—

But . . .

Who knows?

"I'll go, too," I said.

I BeLieve?

■ NaNCY SPRINGeR

Hey hey, Mike Satanik the Evil Deejay here countin' em down on the eve of the big double-oh." It annoyed Mike that he had to orchestrate his historic countdown tonight, because first of all, the real millennium wasn't until 2001, and second of all, the religion freaks who were cranking up the Jesus hysteria refused to understand Jesus was actually born in 4 B.C., so altogether the big double-oh was a crock. But people were stupid. So he had to do his New Millennium's Eve show tonight.

He forced fake-yokel energy into his voice. "Wazoo, ain't that a hoot? I ain't talking the top hundred of the year, people." Speaking to the microphone and the deserted studio, Mike tried to imagine who was listening out there. Teenagers like himself? Kids? Truck drivers? Probably not little old ladies. "I ain't even talking the top hundred of the freaking century, dudes and dudettes. I am gonna be playing for you—hold on to your seats—I am going to be playing Mike Satanik's top one hundred for the mill-freaking-ennium. So hang on tight, we're going for a long freaky ride tonight. Number one hundred, by anonymous monks in brown drag, your basic Gregorian chant. Listen up, here we go!"

He started the CD, slid the microphone volume down to zero, sat back in his chair and sighed. Alone in the studio, not even a producer to talk with. Everybody had some damn party to go to. Okay, fine, he could handle it, and anyway the millennial countdown was his idea and he wouldn't have missed the chance to do it, not for the world.

Just the same, being a deejay was not his idea of a career. He wanted to be a songwriter and a composer. He had been writing songs for years and some of them were almost good, but his pointy-head-like-a-pencil father wouldn't send him to school for music. Said it was too hard to make a living that way. Dad had worked all his life in an office, worried about everything, wanted Mike to "take up something practical," like computers. Right. Sure. And spend the rest of his life in a cubicle trying not to listen to the Musak tinkling from the speakers, wishing. . . .

Of course a lot of people didn't think he had to worry about the rest of his life anyway. Armageddon and all that. Some people were so freaked they weren't even buying green bananas.

As the brief Gregorian chant ended, Mike slid the microphone volume back up to broadcast level. "Hey, whatcha think of that?" he voice-overed. "Whoo-ee, and it only gets better. Anybody hear, did New York fall into the ocean yet? Or is it California that's supposed to go first? Let me know, okay? This is the Millennial Countdown, folks, and here's number ninety-nine: 'Greensleeves,' as sung by the Greenwich Folk Minstrels."

Awesome song. Mike tapped his fingers and hummed along. Ignorant people, all wound up about the year 2000 when a song like "Greensleeves" had been around since God knew when. Not that Mike believed in God. He didn't believe in religion of any kind, not even Satanism. His name really was Mike Satanik, and because of that and his birthday—he had turned thirteen years old on Friday the thirteenth—his friends had started calling him "Evil." Fun nickname to live up to.

Mike's boss drifted in, peered at him suspiciously as if he suspected the kid was up to something, and drifted out again. Nerdy guy. Probably didn't have a party to go to or he wouldn't be here either.

The phone rang. Mike knew the boss wouldn't answer it, and there was nobody else around. This had to be the world's dinkiest radio station, way low-tech, the kind of place that would hire an eighteen-year-old deejay. Mike grabbed the receiver, said "Hold, please," announced the Bach Concerto for two violins in D Minor, and turned back to the phone. "Mike Satanik the Evil Deejay here. Speak to me."

The man's voice sounded tremulous. "Is Felicia there?"

Mike restrained a heavy sigh. Felicia was the deejay for the nighttime warm-and-fuzzy show. Love dedications, call in with your heartthrobby problems, all that. Felicia's favorite song was "I Believe There Are Angels Among Us" for God's sake. Clueless boss kept trying to cater to all kinds instead of finding a niche. Mike didn't worry about the millennium, but he did worry that the station, and his job, wouldn't last six months longer. Mike told the guy, "Not tonight." His countdown was pre-empting Felicia's usual mush.

"Please, can you play something for my wife?" The guy sounded panicky. "She's curled up in the corner crying, she's so scared. Can you—"

"I'm not doing requests, man."

"But—"

"Call the whatchacallit, crisis hotline if she's that bad."

"I tried! It's busy. I can't get through."

"Gotta go." Mike hung up and started a stack of mini-disks, the evening's first batch of ads.

A skirty shadow in the doorway caught his eye. He turned to see Felicia walk in.

"What're *you* doing here?" he yelped, immediately realizing that he sounded somewhat less than polite. But he didn't want her barging in on his countdown.

Felicia smiled with that everlasting and sometimes annoying serenity of hers. "Hello to you, too, Mike."

"Sorry. Hi. What—"

"I forgot I was supposed to loan out Sinatra for somebody's fifties party." She bent to scan the S section of CDs. "You don't need Sinatra, do you?"

"Hell, no." Mike had selected his Millennial Countdown according to his own taste, which definitely did not include Ol' Blue Eyes. He was being kind of chronological about it, and he planned to culminate with Andrew Lloyd Webber, Rusted Root, and Tori Amos.

Felicia rooted among the CDs as Mike watched. He guessed she was a nice looking woman if you could get past the daisy-print dress. She was one of those thirty-something blonds in pink lip gloss, angel pin on her shoulder, sincerity oozing from every healthy, glowing pore. Mike suspected her of being a New-Age freak. She glanced up at him and asked, "How's it going?"

"Fine."

"Any problems?"

"No. Why?"

"I thought it might be a bit crazy tonight. People reacting to the millennium."

Mike said "The millennium is majorly bogus."

"You're not worried? It doesn't mean anything to you?"

Without replying, Mike swiveled his chair to follow up the ads with the pre-recorded station announcement. Behind him he sensed Felicia's silent presence. She seemed to want something from him, but good God, what? Answer an altar call? Maybe he should have told her about her phone call but he didn't want her hanging around. He cued up his next selection—a medieval lute and mandolin piece—and told Felicia over his shoulder, "It means not a rat's ass to me."

She stood up, cradling CDs to her modest bosom, and asked him with a quirk in her voice, "No New Millennium's resolutions?"

Was she joking? Did she have a sense of humor? Mike wasn't sure; he couldn't read her. She made him nervous. He babbled, "Me? No, I don't believe in that crap. January one, whatever year, it's just another day. So, you going to the fifties party?"

"No. I'm going home to be with my husband and daughter." Turning to leave, Felicia smiled at Mike like his mother, like she knew something; he absolutely hated that. "It's not just another day, Mike. It's the turn of the millennium, and it's going to change you."

She waved goodbye and headed out before he could think of a retort.

He stared at the empty doorway, too baffled to swear. Weird goofy witch. Change? What for?

The phone rang.

"Aaaugh!" Mike checked the time left on the lute and mandolin duet, then answered.

A teenage girl's quavering voice this time. "Is Felicia there?"

"No." Thank God. "This is the—"

The girl started to cry. Mike hung up. At once the phone rang again. He grabbed it, yelled, "Hold!" and cued up Vivaldi's *Four Seasons* before barking, "Okay, I suppose you want Felicia?"

"Jesus," the woman whimpered.

"You want Jesus?"

"I—saw! In the sky."

Uh-huh. One of those. Careful, now. Mike droned, "You saw Jesus in the sky?"

"On the TV. Times Square." The woman seemed to be hyperventilating; she could barely speak. "Please," she begged, weeping. "Please. Is Felicia there?"

During the next hour and a half, both phone lines rang without ceasing. The glowing Christ-figure was aurora borealis plus mass hysteria, the scientists kept saying, but half the Times Square crowd had fainted or fallen into fits and people all over the place were crying and screaming. Mike took approximately a call a minute from frightened weepy people requesting Felicia's audio comfort, and he grew so hassled he suffered dead air between the Purcel fugue and Handel's *Water Music,* which he hastily substituted for the "Hallelujah Chorus" because he didn't want to start some sort of riot. Okay, Felicia was right about this night being crazy, but only because people were such idiots. God, this could get worse than that stunt Orson Welles pulled—*War of the Worlds* or whatever—and just as he thought it, a teenage boy called, panicked, seeing UFOs. His parents were out at some party, he didn't know where. Please, Mr. Evil Deejay, interrupt the program and tell them to come home.

Mike slammed down the phone, invoked a nice long Mozart sonata to fill a chunk of air, and went looking for his useless boss. He wanted permission to turn off the phone, which was against station policy. Or if not that, he wanted the boss to pick up the damn calls.

He found the guy passed out on the floor in the front office with a bottle lying by his hand, vodka dribbling on the cheap carpet—not that there was much left to dribble.

"Jesus!" Mike exclaimed more in wonder than in anger. He peered at the boss—yeah, the jerk was breathing okay. Mike trotted back to the studio.

"Okay, to heck with it," he muttered. "I won't answer the damn phone anymore."

As he reached to pull the plug, however, the phone rang. Mike screeched, "Aaaak!" but prompted by a lifetime of Pavlovian conditioning he picked up.

"Mike?" It was his mom's voice. Taken by surprise, he missed a beat and didn't answer.

"Michael?" She sounded upset, like the others, though she had the quiver in her voice under more control. His own mother? God, this couldn't be happening.

"Yeah, what?" He realized he sounded a bit distraught himself.

"Your father's in the hospital. Can you get away?"

"Huh? *Dad?* What happened?"

"He pulled some woman out of a wrecked car and then he had chest pain. They're monitoring his heart, and—"

"Mom, I don't know if I can find a sub!"

"Well, if you can't, you stay. Your dad wouldn't want you walking out on a job."

"Is . . . is he going to be okay?"

"The doctors won't really say, but I think so. I think he's scared, though." God, now his mother had that same know-it-all quirk in her voice as Felicia. "He told me to tell you he loves you."

Mike's mouth opened on its own and got stuck that way. He couldn't speak.

"Michael?"

"Uh."

"Your father said to tell you if he gets through this we'll work out something about music school."

Mike felt his heart ache and earthquake, all the tectonic plates inside him shifting and rearranging, whole new continents of self being formed. He heard somebody, seemed to be him, say, "He doesn't have to."

"Well, that's how he feels. Mike, if you could get over here . . . isn't there anybody you can call?"

"I'll try. Mom, you hang in, okay?"

She said okay and goodbye. Mike sat staring, then realized he had committed yet more dead air. He grabbed a CD, didn't even notice what it was, and got it going. The phone rang again, both lines lit up at once. He hung up on whoever it was and dialed Felicia's number to see if she could come in and take over for him.

"Hello?" It was the hubby.

"This is Mike from the station. Is Felicia there?"

"No, she's not."

"Where is she?" She should have been home an hour ago. With an effort Mike softened his tone. "I've got to talk to her. It's an emergency."

"She's an emergency herself. She was in an accident," the hubby said.

"What?"

"She got forced off the road by some drunk and rolled

her car and it caught on fire. It was a miracle she wasn't killed." The guy's voice had that same caring calmness as Felicia's. He was the first calm person Mike had talked to on the phone all night. "An older man came by and pulled her out just in time. She has minor burns, some lacerations, and a broken collarbone. She's in the hospital overnight for observation."

In the background Mike heard a little girl's voice say anxiously, "Mommy okay?"

Mike could hear the father reply, "Yes, honey, Mommy's going to be fine. An angel came to help Mommy."

Mike hung up and sat staring at the studio wall. God, and the real millennium wasn't until 2001. He wondered what might happen to him then. He realized that he had played Led Zeppelin's "Stairway to Heaven," of all things, probably messing with some religious people's minds in the process, and it was ending. Dead air. He sat, not caring. The phone rang. He answered it.

"Is there any way I can get in touch with Felicia?" It sounded like the same panicky guy who had started off the evening for him, the one with the wife curled in the corner.

"Just a minute," Mike said. "Hold on."

He called the hospital cardiac unit and asked a nurse to tell his mother he couldn't find a sub and would she please listen to him on the radio. "Actually, she already is," the nurse said.

"I should have known," Mike said, hearing his own voice waver just like all those other voices tonight, damn it. He took a deep breath. "How's my dad?"

"He's doing just fine."

After he hung up, Mike hunted for the CD he wanted. It took him a minute to find it, because it wasn't one he would ordinarily play, ever. But he located it, then swiveled to address the microphone and the unknown listeners out there somewhere in the darkness.

"This is, um, this is Mike the deejay," he said. "Tell you what, let's forget the countdown. I've been getting a lot of requests and I'm starting to think that's more important. So all you people who've been calling in, stay tuned, okay? Or anybody else out there, give me a call and let me know what I can do for you. But first there's a song I need to play and I want to dedicate it to my dad and mom."

He cued up his selection and turned back to the phone, where his caller was still on hold. "Hi. Is your wife any better?"

"No. No, she's totally freaked. Is there anything you can play—"

"It's on right now," Mike said.

Then he took the next phone call. "Yeah, I know you're scared. Lots of people are scared, but listen, God is good, right? So why should anything bad happen? Yeah, I just have a feeling it's going to be okay. Sure, I'll find something to play for you."

As he hunted through Felicia's stash of comforting singles, through a process he did not pretend to understand the words and sweet melody of his dedication floated through the night to his mother at his father's bedside, the woman crying in the corner, maybe Felicia's little girl, maybe the teenage boy scared and alone at home, maybe a truck driver somewhere scanning the sky, maybe even a little old lady with her cat on her lap. Many more people than he would ever know.

I believe there are angels among us . . .

HORIZON

■ mICHaeL caDNUm

mom didn't want me to do this.
She had told me the drive
was a bad idea, giving the
deadly winter fogs as the main reason. "People
are always being killed," she'd said.

This is a typical Mom way of putting
things. "Disaster is always striking," she'll say.
She supervises telephone sales of computer
software, providing technical advice to people
she will never see.

This noon, three days after the beginning
of the year—the start of the century, the

flash-bang liftoff of a new millennium, I was the same as blind. I wanted to make a fresh beginning, start the future all over again, but now the white-out visibility slowed me down, my grip on the steering wheel so hard it hurt.

The tule fog was an excuse of Mom's, a way of keeping me from visiting him. But I knew my mother had other reasons for coming close to forbidding me from taking this trip.

I had never driven so far from home, my new driver's license in the purse Mom had given me for Christmas, custom made burgundy cordovan. The leather smell filled the car in the whispery breeze of the car heater. I should have known that Mom's comments about disaster would apply directly to me. I was sure I was about to die.

I crept in behind a big truck in the slow lane, a white barn on wheels, the corners tipped with points of red light. I leaned forward to wipe the condensation off the windshield with my sweater sleeve, remembering with sudden clarity all the reports I had heard every winter, dozens of cars accordioned, forty or fifty vehicles creamed all over the interstate, the motorists fog-blind, just like me.

The truck was the color of the damp that closed around us. I was cold despite the Sentra's heater dial, cranked to the max, my breath coming hard. The green freeway signs passed slowly overhead, dark ghosts I could hardly make out, MODESTO NEXT THREE EXITS. I had a letter from him in my purse, months old, folded and refolded so often it was coming apart, directions to his house in his bold, irregular handwriting.

Mom wouldn't miss me until after five when she got home from her last business meeting, but I wished this veteran little Sentra had a car phone. I was praying out loud that I would make it through the sudden swerve and bob of vehicles, trucks and low-slung Detroit two-doors merging with the through traffic.

Every detail cleared for a few heartbeats, the sun brightening, a lean-faced man in a Stetson drinking from a thermos in the pickup one lane over. Then the fog wiped it all out, replaced the view of freeway traffic with zero visibility. Less than two hours from the San Francisco Bay area, I had left a landscape of urban neighborhoods and shopping areas, and I had entered a damp, naked version of the American West.

I had called him that morning, said I wanted to see him, and he sounded surprised. "Oh, really?" he had said, taking almost too long to follow up with, "That's wonderful, Cerise. Really nice of you." It was as though he was the only person I knew who wasn't eager to make a new start with the millennium.

The Central Valley suburban sprawl of Modesto was

behind me somewhere, swallowed and digested by the solid mist. The big truck loomed steadily ahead, pink chips of light, fog beading on the windshield. They say you can only be scared for so long, after awhile you get used to it.

It's not true. I almost didn't see COTTONWOOD RD and nearly drove past the off-ramp. All four tires whined as I swung the steering wheel.

I left the freeway behind. I drove carefully down a two-lane highway, the road surface blotchy with water and pot-hole repairs.

The fog was more transparent here, black barns and gray horses across winter-bare fields. A creek snaked across a landscape that looked like calendar art of rural poverty, an ancient school bus on wooden struts across a pasture, like an ark.

"Keep your eyes on the odometer," he had said.

Fifteen and a half miles, exactly.

There wasn't another dwelling near it, a single story blue stucco house with a black shingle roof. The driveway crackled under the tires. When I was out of the car, the cold had me. Across the gray gravel a screen door creaked.

He was whiter than I remembered him, white-haired, with long pale arms. He let the screen door close behind him carefully, so it made no sound. He stepped to the edge of the porch.

"Jesus, I was worried," he said.

We hugged, like actors in an early rehearsal, not getting it quite right. His voice was husky. "I made lemonade for you. By hand, with real lemons."

It was sour and too cold, but I drank. I put down my glass and licked my lips, like a child. I had not seen my father in eight years, since just after my ninth birthday. They had not let me go to the trial. Mom said she never wanted to set eyes on him again.

"Want another glass?"

He held his head aslant to catch my words, like a man going deaf in one ear. He filled my glass again, but did not pour himself any more. He put the pitcher back into the refrigerator, moving slowly. I knew he was fifteen years older that Mom, but now for the first time I understood something about age, how it worked against a man who used to show me how to choke-up on the bat, get the bunt down and run like crazy, demonstrating, sprinting all the way to the trashcan lid, first base.

Outside, the sun was winning and the fog was giving up. There was a horizon, flat, spiked with fence posts, far-off naked trees.

"It's all mine," he said, gesturing. "As far as you want to see."

It was odd the way he put it. As though a person might not want to see, might prefer to stay inside, reading, watching television, not looking out. I had assumed he had money—he sent Mom's bank an electronic transfer every month.

"Be careful," he said. "Rattlers hibernate in the squirrel holes."

He was trying out a Western, outdoorsy way of speaking that was unfamiliar to me. "It's beautiful," I said.

He walked ahead of me. "You find cattle bones out here." The space between us diminished his voice, made it seem far away, and at the same time made each step distinct, a crackle of white weed. "They make a funny odor when you pick them up—a sour smell, like plaster." Maybe he wasn't trying to talk in this country-western accent. Maybe he always had, and I had forgotten.

"You've always written letters," he said at last. "You're good about that." Then, sensing me about to stall and get emotional, or begin to ask the question I had come here to ask, he added, "I had some money when I got out of Lompoc. My parents set up a trust account before they died."

The mention of the prison, the Men's Colony near San Luis Obispo, made me look down, careful to avoid the

dried sparklers of grass seed, the winter-wet soil just beginning to give life to the weedy field.

"Listen," he said.

I heard nothing but my father's wristwatch.

"It's quiet," I offered.

"I love it. Look here," he said, nudging a crumbling
piece of wood with his boot. "Used to be a cattle trough. Off
over there are some of the bones I told you about."

We found them, ribs scattered wide. We stood in the
scattered chalk remnants of a beast. The creature had been
a steer, I imagined, but it could have been a dinosaur, or
even a giant human. "I wonder sometimes," he said, "what
killed them."

I called Mom at three minutes after five.

I spoke breezily, getting all the information out at once,
just the opposite of the way she communicates. I expected
her to be Mom of Ice, cold with anger.

Instead she was quiet, and I could sense her being careful, picking the words that would do the least harm. She
asked how the fog had been, and how the car had handled.
I reassured her, lying a little, saying the fog hadn't been
that bad.

I wished my dad wasn't in the kitchen next to me, getting the lid off a can with an electric opener.

"It's probably safer than risking the drive again," she agreed wearily, when she heard my plan.

Then I heard her say. "Let me talk to him."

I left the house as he took the phone and said, "Hello there, Ruthie," sounding the way he used to, coming home with an armload of groceries, laundry, newspapers. He had always carried more than he could, items falling from his grasp as he hurried to put the load down.

"Don't worry about her, Ruthie," he was saying. "She'll be fine."

We had tuna macaroni for supper. I told him all about Mom's office on Solano Avenue, where she helped to decide how to sell things like a leopard-spotted computer carrier.

But when I told him about Mom's brother, his new pilot's license, her parents, their new house in La Jolla, he nodded without looking at me. I realized that I was telling Dad about people who had encouraged Mom through the divorce and afterward. Their names didn't mean very much to him anymore.

He said he helped people prepare their tax returns, and did some consulting work with a real estate firm in Madera, "amortizing loans, showing widows how to refinance their duplexes."

"So you do get out," I said. I meant he did have friends, but something about the way I said it made him smile.

"What's funny?"

"You make it sound like I'm a caged animal," he laughed.

That night I woke, startled at the quiet.

I walked to the front door and opened it. The soap-pale field lay like the landscape of another planet, a planet people could inhabit only at great peril.

Tomorrow, I promised myself, I would tell my father how difficult it had been for mom, for both of us, getting ready to go to school, ignoring the newspaper articles on the kitchen table, the black headlines on page six, page nineteen, never front page news but persistent, ugly.

I stepped across the porch. The air was still, cold, but the fog was gone. The fine black line at the edge of what could be seen was the road. I waited for a long time, and no cars passed on the two-lane.

Wrong, I wanted to say. You *wronged* us. If you were innocent, you should have fought harder. You wouldn't have let them take you to prison.

My father's light was on when I tiptoed back into the house. His bedroom door was open, and I could see his knee, clad in blue pajamas. He cleared his throat, a sound that touched me from my childhood. He lowered a book to his knee, closing it around his finger, and sat still, at the end of his bed.

In the morning it was clear, white winter sun out each window.

He said, "I heard you up in the night."

I drank some cranberry juice. "The quiet woke me."

I have always hated mornings, having to talk and act cheerful, so early everything the sun touches hurts your eyes. For a moment I wished it was foggy again.

He turned and pried the lid off a can of coffee. "I couldn't sleep either," he said.

We ate breakfast, toast without butter, oatmeal with brown sugar.

Afterward he showed me how to kick-start a cute little red Kawasaki motorcycle, running alongside the machine for a while before I picked up speed. I left him behind, hands on his hips, smiling and breathing hard.

I circled back over the hummocks and tufts of the just-beginning green, steering pretty well for someone who had never been on a motorcycle in her life, although I killed the engine when I tried to speed up. For the first time I could see the way he used to be, excited, encouraging, clapping his hands. Maybe it was all I had come for.

The entire East Bay had followed the nagging story about a realtor and neighborhood kids. Sexual assault on a minor. My dad said it never happened, but he had plea-bargained a guilty plea, lewd conduct. Because, he had explained, the lawyers were draining Mom and me of everything we owned.

Mom says goodbyes are little deaths.

I wanted to leave—it was the kind of moment when words run out of strength and there's nothing to say. After we hugged and I started the car, he turned to go inside. He held the screen door like the cover to a book, between his thumb and forefinger. The Sentra's motor was cold, and I had to let it idle, blue steam and exhaust billowing in the pale sunlight.

I felt superstitious suddenly, so early in a new year, a whole new chapter, a thousand years long, waiting to fill up with names and dates. I rolled down the window and I wished him a happy new year.

He came out, and made his way across the lawn again, his head cocked to hear what I was saying.

There was no fog, only a distant haze against the hills.

I stopped for gas beside the freeway. I unhooked the gas gun. A guy my age in a huge zip-up jacket that made him big around as a bear came out of the garage bay to look at me. It was cold but clear, and the air smelled of oil, old grease. I could see the handprint in the road grime where my father had touched the car, leaning in to return my wish for the new year.

It was my policy never to pee in a restroom in a place like that, even though I started off in that direction, around the corner, stopping when I reminded myself that I probably had sufficient bladder strength to make it to Oakland. A stand of daisies beside a stack of tires shivered in the wind of passing trucks.

I was standing there along the side of the gas station when I heard the chime of the cage. Immediately I knew I was in the presence of something I did not want to see.

Two eyes looked. They blinked.

"Does that creature ever get a chance to get out?" I handed him a twenty dollar bill.

"It would go right for your eyes." He added, "To it, you're just a walking piece of meat."

He handed me the change bill on a plastic tray, an odd nicety, as though this use-worn Chevron station thought of itself as a stylish place.

The guy looked at me sideways, perhaps secretly eager to argue with this strange young woman, maybe as a way of flirting, or at least getting the conversation to last a little longer.

"What do you suppose he thinks about?" I asked.

"I don't think it thinks." He looked away, though, and shrugged. He said gently, "He sleeps most of the time."

I took a drink of ice-cold water at the Coke machine, but I wanted only to see the bird again. The bottom of the cage was a crowd of pink bones.

He was dangerous, I knew. I could be hurt.

I touched the side of the cage. He looked at me, not a classic horned owl, but a white-faced barn owl, a powder puff with a hooked beak. I slipped my finger into the cage. I wiggled it.

I held my breath. If he struck me, and drew blood, it would be what I deserved.

tomorrow

■ NataLie BaBBitt

the morning Mr. Rummage went straight up into the sky, everyone made a big fuss, and the television and newspaper reporters wanted the whole story. Mrs. Rummage was willing to tell them whatever she could, but she said straight off that they needed to understand about Mr. Rummage: he was likely to have ideas now and again—she stressed the word "ideas"—and sometimes he got carried away. The only thing that made it different this time, she said, was that he'd got carried a lot farther away than usual. Even the

Rummage children agreed with that. There were three of them—Roy, Rose, and Roger—and mostly they didn't agree about anything, but this time they were having too good a time to disagree, what with their father going straight up like that and the TV cameras and reporters all over the backyard.

Mrs. Rummage described how things had started, as well as she could remember. One day—it must have been a weekend because Mr. Rummage was home from his job at the ladder factory—one day, completely out of the blue, he started singing an old song nobody ever sings anymore. It had some lines about giving yourself a pat on the back, and in one place the words went like this:

. . . and nobody knows what's going to happen tomorrow.

He went around singing it so much that at last Mrs. Rummage asked him about it. She said, "What made you dig up that old thing?" And Mr. Rummage said, "Mildred,"—that was Mrs. Rummage's name—"Mildred, just think how nice it would be if people *did* know what was going to happen tomorrow!"

Mrs. Rummage was a practical person who always saw straight through to the bottom of things. "I don't think it would be nice at all," she said to Mr. Rummage. "What if you knew a bus was going to run into you? You'd be up all night, the night before, worrying."

"I wasn't thinking of something like that, exactly," said Mr. Rummage. "Not like getting run into by a bus. I was thinking more in general terms. You know. Like, will tomorrow be good or not so good."

"But how could you decide which was which?" said Mrs. Rummage. "Take rain, for instance. Good for a garden, not good for a picnic."

"Mildred," said Mr. Rummage, "you don't see the point." And before she could say anything more, he went off to the garage and started messing around with tools.

The next thing that happened was, a little while later, Mr. Rummage got out of bed in the middle of the night and went down to the living room to think about whether or not it would be nice to know about tomorrow. He decided it probably *would* be nice. But you'd have to find a way to be sure of the prediction. Mr. Rummage didn't have much confidence in fortune tellers, and anyway, didn't they mostly talk about the distant future? He wasn't even wondering about a week from next Thursday. All he was wondering about was tomorrow.

It was cool in the living room, due to the fact that the furnace was always turned down at night, and Mr. Rummage sat there so long thinking about predictions that at last he began to shiver. And he could feel his throat getting sore. So he pulled a coat on over his pajamas and went outside and down through the park to the all-night drugstore to get himself some cough drops. The thing that was important, said Mrs. Rummage to the reporters, happened right after that: Mr. Rummage was on his way back when he went by a very old man sitting on a bench. "Hey," said the very old man, pointing to the eastern horizon. "Looky there."

Mr. Rummage looked and saw a pink and golden glow spreading out low behind the trees. "Oh, yes," he said politely, walking on. "Very pretty."

"Pretty?" said the very old man. *"Pretty? That's not what it's about. What it's about is, here comes tomorrow."*

When Mr. Rummage heard this, he stopped in the middle of the sidewalk and stared at the horizon. "Well, I'll be!" he said. "I see what you mean."

"Sure," said the very old man. "I been waitin' all night for tomorrow and—finally! Here it comes, waltzing in, right on time!"

Mr. Rummage went on home and took a cough drop, which helped his sore throat, but he couldn't sleep because now there was even more to think about than there'd been before. Like, for instance, when did tomorrow turn into today? If you wanted to know whether tomorrow was going to be good or not so good, wouldn't you have to look at it while it was still tomorrow? The whole question made him dizzy.

He woke up Mrs. Rummage and told her all this, but

she couldn't see anything in it. Or so she said to the reporters. "I couldn't see anything in it," she told them. "But it seemed to me it might be a good idea if I kept my eye on Mr. Rummage, just in case." They asked her, "Just in case what?" but she clammed up on that particular point. Instead, she told them about the last little piece that had happened just before Mr. Rummage started getting carried away.

This piece was something Mr. Rummage overheard the next day at the ladder factory. There was a new ladder coming out that was going to slide open in such a way that you could stretch it out to twenty feet if you wanted to, and everyone was talking about it. "Yessir," someone said, "you can see all the way into the middle of next week from the top of a rig like that."

When Mr. Rummage heard this, he turned pale and his eyes opened very wide. "That's it!" he said to himself. "That's how." And he wished he could go home and tell Mrs. Rummage.

Then, as luck would have it, his boss came by and said, "What's the matter, Rummage? You're kind of pale, and your eyes look funny."

"I didn't get much sleep last night," said Mr. Rummage, who wasn't ready to talk about the rest of it yet.

"Go home and lie down," said his boss. "We can't have you getting sick."

Mr. Rummage went happily home and cornered Mrs. Rummage in the kitchen, where she was chopping vegetables. "Mildred," he said, "I've got it."

"What've you got?" she asked. "Mumps? The flu? You're pale and your eyes look funny."

"Mildred, be quiet and listen," said Mr. Rummage. "Here's the whole situation. I've made up my mind. It *would* be nice to know what tomorrow will be like. So, the thing is, there are places out east where tomorrow's already started. All you have to do is get up high enough to look down at it before it gets as far as here, and then you can tell what it'll be like!"

"You've got a fever," said Mrs. Rummage. "Sit down and I'll get you some aspirin."

But Mr. Rummage didn't want any aspirin. He put on old clothes and went out to the garage to examine his ladder collection. He didn't have the new one that opened out to twenty feet, of course, because the factory wasn't ready with that one yet. But he did have a nice ten-footer.

Along about 4:30 next morning, while it was still dark, Mr. Rummage woke up Mrs. Rummage. "I'm going over to the park now," he told her. "Don't worry. It's just that I have to do some research and the park's the best place. I'll be back in time for breakfast." He put his old clothes on again, and then, with the ladder wobbling around under his arm, he headed straight for the park. He picked out what seemed like the tallest tree, leaned the ladder against it so he could get up onto a lower branch, and then he climbed until he was as near the top as a grown man could get.

It was a lovely, clear night, with just a hint of dawn on the eastern horizon, and Mr. Rummage settled himself in a good place where he could watch without too many leaves getting in the way. Slowly, the hint of dawn spread into a pink and golden glow that widened and widened until at last there was enough light to see by.

Mr. Rummage studied as much of the land as he could, but there was nothing. Nothing at all to base a prediction on. Just some buildings here and there, and lots of other trees. And then the sun came up and it wasn't tomorrow anymore. Mr. Rummage frowned and shook his head. "Still, this is only the first experiment," he said to himself. "It's clear I'm not up near high enough, for one thing. And I ought to have a good, strong pair of binoculars."

The next day, Mr. Rummage went back to his job at the ladder factory, but at lunchtime he bought some binoculars, and then he called on the Reverend Dr. Mendenhall and asked for permission to go up into the steeple of the church when nighttime came. "I want to see what things look like from the top just before the sun comes up," he explained, hoping there would be questions, because now he felt ready to talk about his idea. But the Reverend Dr. Mendenhall wasn't curious. All he said was, "Oh. Certainly. Help yourself." And he gave Mr. Rummage the key.

The church steeple was a little better than the tree had been. Mr. Rummage saw the light spread out maybe as much as thirty seconds before he'd have seen it if he'd been on the ground. But even with the new binoculars, thirty seconds wasn't long enough, not by half.

Next morning at breakfast, Mr. Rummage said to Mrs. Rummage and the children, "Somehow I've just got to get up higher."

"Maybe you should try the top of the Scruffendorf Building," said Roy. "They told us in school it's the tallest building in town."

"That's a good idea, Roy," said Mr. Rummage. "I'll look into it."

Mr. Rummage looked into it and ended up spending the night on top of the Scruffendorf Building. Along about 3 A.M., it rained like the dickens, so it wasn't the best night he'd ever spent. However, he managed to keep the binoculars dry, and the sky cleared just before dawn. This time he was up high enough to see the light spread out over a big farm a few miles away to the east, and he was sure the roosters who lived there would be crowing a little bit sooner than roosters on farms closer to town. But he couldn't prove it, and anyway, what use were roosters? Near or far, they all said the same thing every time they crowed, didn't they? Something like, "Time to get up"? It was hard to imagine a rooster knowing what kind of a day it was going to be and putting that into a morning announcement.

Still, thinking about roosters gave Mr. Rummage an idea. Flying! That was the ticket, he said to Mrs. Rummage and the children when he came home for breakfast.

"Roosters can't fly," said Roy.

"That's neither here nor there, Roy," said Mr. Rummage. "What I'm saying is, I think the right thing to do is catch a night flight somewhere in some direction where I can look out a window that faces east. It won't cost much. These red-eye flights are pretty cheap. And tomorrow's Saturday, so I won't miss a minute at the factory."

That night, Mr. Rummage went out to the airport and waited around and then, along about 5:00 in the morning, he got on a flight for Akron. The idea was mostly a good one, because he was up plenty high, all right. But when the proper moment came, the plane kept moving so fast that he couldn't stay focused on the land under it long enough to see anything.

When he got home again, he explained this to Mrs. Rummage but she wasn't sympathetic. "Thank goodness that airplane *did* keep moving," she told him. "I'd hate to think what would've happened otherwise!" Which was a good point, he had to admit. But he was stumped as to what to do next.

"The thing is," said Roy—Roy was in fifth grade and

kept his eyes and ears open, so he didn't miss much—"The thing is, it'll all be simple when they figure out a way to go faster than the speed of light."

"How's that, Roy?" asked Mr. Rummage.

"It's like this," said Roy. "All you'd have to do is travel faster than the speed of light, see, and then when you got where you were going, you could turn around and watch yourself coming, and watch what was happening along the way."

"Well!" said Mr. Rummage. "My goodness, Roy! That *is* a notion. But I don't think anyone will ever go faster than the speed of light."

"That's what they used to say about flying to the moon," said Roy.

This, of course, was true. But it was not helpful. Mr. Rummage sent Roy away to rake the backyard and sat down to settle his thoughts by reading the first volume of the encyclopedia, the volume with A and B in it. And that was when he found his solution.

In the encyclopedia, under BALLOON, was a long account about a couple of brothers over in France two hundred years ago—Montgolfier was their name—who made a bunch of balloons out of paper and filled them up with smoke and they actually flew! And carried people! Way up in the sky, more than three thousand feet high!

"That's the ticket, then," said Mr. Rummage to himself. All of a sudden, he felt very calm. "A balloon can be tied to the ground with a long rope, so it won't go any-where. And if you're up three thousand feet, you almost *will* be able to see into the middle of next week." But could he make a paper balloon and fill it with smoke and ride it up into the sky? Why not? If a couple of brothers over in France two hundred years ago could do it, then a person from nowadays could do it, even if he didn't have a brother.

Mrs. Rummage drew a long breath here and looked around at all the reporters and television cameras. "That was six weeks ago," she said. "And now—well—I don't know what else to tell you. He's got the balloon tied to the porch railing here. You can see the rope for yourselves, tight as a harpstring. And you can see the remains of the stuff he burned to make the smoke, right there in the wash-tub. He's up there. He went up along about five o'clock this morning. So—I guess you'll have to wait till he comes down again if you've got any questions."

"Now wait a minute," said one of the reporters. "How did he know how to make a paper balloon?"

"I can't say," said Mrs. Rummage. "I wasn't here to watch. He quit his job at the ladder factory so he could work on it, and I went part-time down at Bigbee's. In the glove and scarf department. Just to help out. But I can tell you this much: He had a lot of help from the children. Roy's in fifth grade, you know. He can do a whole lot of differ-ent things. And Rose and Roger are both really good with scissors and paste."

So they all looked at each other, and up into the brightening morning sky, and they fidgeted and tramped around on the grass, and then someone standing near the porch railing said, "Hey! Looks like he's on his way!" For the rope had begun to go a little limp, and then it went limper, until at last there came the balloon, basket first, drifting slowly, slowly, down out of the clouds, down to the treetops, down to the rooftops, and at last, as everyone hurried to get out of the way, down to exactly where it had begun. And here was Mr. Rummage, in his old clothes, with the binoculars slung around his neck. He looked tired. And a little sad.

The reporters crowded around with their notebooks and cameras, all talking at once, until finally someone said it so loud that everyone else kept still and waited for the answer: "What did you see up there, Mr. Rummage? Did you look at tomorrow? Did you find out if today is going to be good or not?"

Mr. Rummage climbed out of the basket just in time for the balloon to give a big sigh and slump over sideways. "Ladies and gentlemen," said Mr. Rummage, "it's beautiful up there. I saw that first glow spread out a long time before you saw it down here. I saw it spread out clear over to Zanesville, over a whole lot of farms and little towns and hills full of trees and places like that. I saw bunches of birds. And I saw some people on motorcycles headed north on Route 77. At least, I *think* it was people on motorcycles. But

I'm afraid that, even with binoculars, even with it's still being tomorrow I was looking at, I didn't find out anything about today."

"Why not?" asked someone. "What went wrong, do you think?"

Mr. Rummage took off the binoculars and handed them to Mrs. Rummage. "I don't know for sure," he said. "All I can think of is, maybe if you get up high enough to see tomorrow coming, you're up too high to see what it's saying about today."

The reporters wrote it all down anyway, and there was a lot more picture taking, even some shots of Mrs. Rummage and the children giving Mr. Rummage a hug. The whole thing was on the evening news on television, and in the evening papers, and no one said Mr. Rummage was a kook. They were all of them too impressed about the paper balloon. But there was no denying the fact that Mr. Rummage was sad. He kept thinking there ought to have been more than this. "And now I haven't got a job, even," he said to Mrs. Rummage, though he waited to say this till the children were in bed, so as not to have them worry.

"Never mind," said Mrs. Rummage. "It'll all work out. You'll see. You'll feel better when you've had a good night's rest."

They went to bed, then, and Mr. Rummage tried to go to sleep. He probably did doze a little here and there. But along about 5:00 A.M. he got out of bed and went down to the living room where he sat and thought for a little while and then pulled on his coat and went for a walk in the park. And there, on the same bench, he saw the very old man. "Well? Was I right about it or what?" said the very old man.

"Right about what?" said Mr. Rummage.

"About tomorrow," said the very old man. "I told you I was waiting for it, didn't I? And then there it was. It's probably going to come again, here pretty soon."

"Probably?" said Mr. Rummage. "It *always* comes."

"Sonny," said the very old man, "the most anyone can say is, it's always come *so* far. But you can't say more than that. This being the case, it's good when you see that light showing up over there one more time. That feller in that paper balloon—did you read about him?—he was a kook. Who cares what kind of a day it's going to be? What matters is if there's even going to *be* a day." And then he took Mr. Rummage's arm. "Looky," he said. "Here it comes." And once again, as they watched together, a pink and golden streak appeared, and widened, and spread, and right before their eyes another tomorrow waltzed in, right on time.

Mr. Rummage looked at the sun coming up and he felt much better. He took the very old man home with him for breakfast, where everyone liked him a lot, and Roy even talked to him about going faster than the speed of light. And later on that day, Mr. Rummage got his old job back and more besides, because someone in the advertising department at the ladder factory had had a great idea: a shot of Mr. Rummage going up in his balloon, with a caption that said, YOU CAN GET UP PRETTY HIGH THIS WAY BUT IT'S HARD TO HAMMER. TRY ONE OF OUR LADDERS INSTEAD. It ran in all the newspapers, and even went live on TV, and orders for the new twenty-footer went very nicely because of it. So Mr. Rummage was a little bit famous there for a while. But he didn't let it carry him away.

the three-century woman

■ RICHARD peck

I guess if you live long enough," my mom said to Aunt Gloria, "you get your fifteen minutes of fame."

Mom was on the car phone to Aunt Gloria. The minute Mom rolls out of the garage, she's on her car phone. It's state of the art and better than her car.

We were heading for Whispering Oaks to see my Great-Grandmother Breckenridge, who's lived there since I was a little girl. They call it an Elder Care Facility. Needless to say, I hated going.

The reason for Great-Grandma's fame is that she was born in 1899. Now it's January 2001. If you're one of those people who claim the new century begins in 2001, not 2000, even you have to agree that Great-Grandma Breckenridge has lived in three centuries. This is her claim to fame.

We waited for a light to change along by Northbrook Mall, and I gazed fondly over at it. Except for the Multiplex, it was closed because of New Year's Day. I have a severe mall habit. But I'm fourteen, and the mall is the place without homework. Aunt Gloria's voice filled the car.

"If you take my advice," she told Mom, "you'll keep those Whispering Oaks people from letting the media in to interview Grandma. Interview her my foot! Honestly. She doesn't even know where she is, let alone how many centuries she's lived in. The poor old soul. Leave her in peace. She's already got one foot in the—"

"Gloria, your trouble is you have no sense of history." Mom gunned across the intersection. "You got a C in History."

"I was sick a lot that year," Aunt Gloria said.

"Sick of history," Mom murmured.

"I heard that," Aunt Gloria said.

They bickered on, but I tuned them out. Then when we turned in at Whispering Pines, a sound truck from IBC-TV was blocking the drive.

"Good grief," Mom murmured. "TV."

"I told you," Aunt Gloria said, but Mom switched her off. She parked in a frozen rut.

"I'll wait in the car," I said. "I have homework."

"Get out of the car," Mom said.

If you get so old you have to be put away, Whispering Oaks isn't that bad. It smells all right, and a Christmas tree glittered in the lobby. A real tree. On the other hand, you have to push a red button to unlock the front door. I guess it's to keep the inmates from escaping, though Great-Grandma Breckenridge wasn't going anywhere and hadn't for twenty years.

When we got to her wing, the hall was full of camera crews and a woman from the suburban newspaper with a notepad.

Mom sighed. It was like that first day of school when you think you'll be okay until the teachers learn your name. Stepping over a cable, we stopped at Great-Grandma's door, and they were on to us.

"Who are you people to Mrs. Breckenridge?" the newspaperwoman said. "I want names."

These people were seriously pushy. And the TV guy was wearing more makeup than Mom. It dawned on me that they couldn't get into Great-Grandma's room without her permission. Mom turned on them.

"Listen, you're not going to be interviewing my grandmother," she said in a quiet bark. "I'll be glad to tell you anything you want to know about her, but you're not going in there. She's got nothing to say, and . . . she needs a lot of rest."

"Is it Alzheimer's?" the newswoman asked. "Because we're thinking Alzheimer's."

"Think what you want," Mom said. "But this is as far as you get. And you people with the camera and the light, you're not going in there either. You'd scare her to death, and then I'd sue the pants off you."

They pulled back.

But a voice came wavering out of Great-Grandma's room. Quite an eerie, echoing voice.

"Let them in!" the voice said.

It had to be Great-Grandma Breckenridge. Her roommate had died. "Good grief," Mom murmured, and the press surged forward.

Mom and I went in first, and our eyes popped. Great-Grandma was usually flat out in the bed, dozing, with her teeth in a glass and a book in her hand. Today she was bright-eyed and propped up. She wore a fuzzy pink bed jacket. A matching bow was stuck in what remained of her hair.

"Oh for pity's sake," Mom murmured. "They've got her done up like a Barbie doll."

Great-Grandma peered from the bed at Mom. "And who are you?" she asked.

"I'm Ann," Mom said carefully. "This is Megan," she said, meaning me.

"That's right," Great-Grandma said. "At least you know who you are. Plenty around this place don't."

The guy with the camera on his shoulder barged in. The other guy turned on a blinding light.

Great-Grandma blinked. In the glare we noticed she wore a trace of lipstick. The TV anchor elbowed the woman reporter aside and stuck a mike in Great-Grandma's face. Her claw hand came out from under the covers and tapped it.

"Is this thing on?" she inquired.

"Yes, ma'am," the TV anchor said in his broadcasting voice. "Don't you worry about all this modern technology. We don't understand half of it ourselves." He gave her his big, five-thirty news smile and settled on the edge of her bed. There was room for him. She was tiny.

"We're here to congratulate you for having lived in three centuries—for being a Three-Century Woman! A great achievement."

Great-Grandma waved a casual claw. "Nothing to it," she said. "You sure this mike's on? Let's do this in one take."

The cameraman snorted and moved in for a closer shot. Mom stood still as a statue, wondering what was going to come out of Great-Grandma's mouth next.

"Mrs. Breckenridge," the anchor said, "to what do you attribute your long life?"

"I was only married once," Great-Grandma said. "And he died young."

The anchor stared. "Ah. And anything else?"

"Yes. I don't look back. I live in the present."

The camera panned around the room. This was all the present she had, and it didn't look like much.

"You live for the present," the anchor said, looking for an angle, "even now?"

Great-Grandma nodded. "Something's always happening. Last night I fell off the bed pan."

Mom groaned.

The cameraman pulled in for a tighter shot. The anchor seemed to search his mind. You could tell he thought he was a great interviewer, though he had no sense of humor. A tiny smile played around Great-Grandma's wrinkled lips.

"But you've lived through amazing times, Mrs. Breckenridge. And you never think back about them?"

Great-Grandma stroked her chin and considered. "You mean you want to hear something interesting? Like how I lived through the San Francisco earthquake—the big one of oh-six?"

Beside me, Mom stirred. We were crowded over by the dead lady's bed. "You survived the 1906 San Francisco earthquake?" the anchor said.

Great-Grandma gazed at the ceiling, lost in thought.

"I'd have been about seven years old. My folks and I

were staying at that big hotel. You know the one. I slept in a cot at the foot of their bed. In the middle of the night, that room gave a shake, and the chiffonier walked right across the floor. You know what chiffonier is?"

"A chest of drawers?" the anchor said.

"Close enough," Great-Grandma said. "And the pictures flapped on the walls. We had to walk down twelve flights because the elevators didn't work. When we got outside, the streets were ankle-deep in broken glass. You never saw such a mess in your life."

Mom nudged me and hissed: "She's never been to San Francisco. She's never been west of Denver. I've heard her say so."

"Incredible!" the anchor said.

"Truth's stranger than fiction," Great-Grandma said, smoothing her sheet.

"And you never think back about it?"

Great-Grandma shrugged her little fuzzy pink shoulders. "I've been through too much. I don't have time to remember it all. I was on the Hindenburg when it blew up, you know."

Mom moaned, and the cameraman was practically standing on his head for a close-up.

"The Hindenburg?"

"That big gas bag the Germans built to fly over the Atlantic Ocean. It was called a zeppelin. Biggest thing you ever saw—five city blocks long. It was in May of 1937, before your time. You wouldn't remember. My husband and I were coming back from Europe on it. No, wait a minute."

Great-Grandma cocked her head and pondered for the camera.

"My husband was dead by then. It was some other man. Anyway, the two of us were coming back on the Hindenburg. It was smooth as silk. You didn't know you were moving. When we flew in over New York, they stopped the ball game at Yankee Stadium to see us passing overhead."

Great-Grandma paused, caught up in memories.

"And then the Hindenburg exploded," the anchor said, prompting her.

She nodded. "We had no complaints about the trip till then. The luggage was all stacked, and we were coming in at Lakehurst, New Jersey. I was wearing my beige coat— beige or off-white, I forget. Then whoosh! The gondola heated up like an oven, and people peeled out of the windows. We hit the ground and bounced. When we hit again, the door fell off, and I walked out and kept going. When they caught up with me in the parking lot, they wanted to put me in the hospital. I looked down and thought I was wearing a lace dress. The fire had about burned up my coat. And I lost a shoe."

"Fantastic!" the anchor breathed. "What detail!" Behind him the woman reporter was scribbling away on her pad.

"Never," Mom muttered. "Never in her life."

"Ma'am, you are living history!" the anchor said. "In your sensational span of years you've survived two great disasters!"

"Three." Great-Grandma patted the bow on her head. "I told you I'd been married."

"And before we leave this venerable lady," the anchor said, flashing a smile for the camera, "we'll ask Mrs. Breckenridge if she has any predictions for this new twenty-first century ahead of us here in the Dawn of the Millennium."

"Three or four predictions," Great-Grandma said, and paused again, stretching out her airtime. "Number one, taxes will be higher. Number two, it's going to be harder to find a place to park. And number three, a whole lot of people are going to live as long as I have, so get ready for us."

"And with those wise words," the anchor said, easing off the bed, "we leave Mrs. Breck—"

"And one more prediction," she said. "TV's on the way out. Your network ratings are already in the basement. It's all websites now. Son, I predict you'll be looking for work."

And that was it. The light went dead. The anchor, looking shaken, followed his crew out the door. When TV's done with you, they're done with you. "Is that a wrap?" Great-Grandma asked.

But now the woman from the suburban paper was moving in on her. "Just a few more questions, Mrs. Breckenridge."

"Where you from?" Great-Grandma blinked pink-eyed at her.

"The Glenview Weekly Shopper."

"You bring a still photographer with you?" Great-Grandma asked.

"Well, no."

"And you never learned shorthand either, did you?"

"Well . . . no."

"Honey, I only deal with professionals. There's the door."

So then it was just Mom and Great-Grandma and I in the room. Mom planted a hand on her hip. "Grandma. Number one, you've never been to San Francisco. And number two, you never *saw* one of those zeppelin things."

Great-Grandma shrugged. "No, but I can read." She nodded to the pile of books on her nightstand with her spectacles folded on top. "You can pick up all that stuff in books."

"And number three," Mom said. "Your husband didn't die young. I can *remember* Grandpa Breckenridge."

"It was that TV dude in the five-hundred-dollar suit who set me off," Great-Grandma said. "He dyes his hair, did you notice? He made me mad, and it put my nose out of joint. He didn't notice I'm still here. He thought I was nothing but my memories. So I gave him some."

Now Mom and I stood beside her bed.

"I'll tell you something else," Great-Grandma said. "And it's no lie."

We waited, holding our breath to hear. Great-Grandma Breckenridge was pointing her little old bent finger right at me. "You, Megan," she said. "Once upon a time, I was your age. How scary is that?"

Then she hunched up her little pink shoulders and winked at me. She grinned and I grinned. She was just this little withered-up leaf of a lady in the bed. But I felt like giving her a kiss on her little wrinkled cheek, so I did.

"I'll come to see you more often," I told her.

"Call first," she said. "I might be busy." Then she dozed.

aBOut tHe autHORS

AVI is the author of such well-loved books as *The True Confessions of Charlotte Doyle,* recipient of a Newbery Honor Medal in 1991; *Nothing but the Truth,* a Newbery Honor recipient in 1992; *Encounter at Easton,* a 1980 Christopher Award winner; *Poppy,* winner of the 1996 Horn Book/Boston Globe Fiction Award, as well many children's choice award titles. A firm believer that reading is the key to writing, Avi is the founder of Breakfast Serials, a program that encourages kids to read by publishing good books for young people in our nation's newspapers. He lives in Denver, Colorado. For more information on Avi, visit his website: *www.avi-writer.com.*

NATALIE BABBITT began her career illustrating a story written by her husband, Sam. Since then, she has gone on to write and/or illustrate many books for young readers, including *The Devil's Storybook* and *Nellie: A Cat on Her Own.* Natalie is perhaps best known for her classic novels *Kneeknock Rise,* recipient of a Newbery Honor Medal, and *Tuck Everlasting,* an American Library Association Notable Book for Children. She lives in Providence, Rhode Island.

MICHAEL CADNUM's acclaimed novels include *Heat; Breaking the Fall,* nominated for the 1992 Edgar Allen Poe Award for Best Young Adult Mystery; and *In a Dark Wood,* a finalist for the 1999 *Los Angeles Times* Young Adult Book

Award. A former Creative Writing Fellow of the National Endowment of the Arts, Michael has also published several collections of poetry, including *The Cities We Will Never See,* and a picture book for children, *The Lost and Found House.* He lives in Albany, California.

MADELEINE L'ENGLE writes for both adults and young adults, captivating her audiences with fantastic plots and authentic characters. She is the author of the classic *A Wrinkle in Time,* the first title in her five-book Time series, and recipient of the 1963 Newbery Medal. Another book in the series, *A Swiftly Tilting Planet,* received the American Book Award in 1980. Madeleine says she has written "ever since she could hold a pencil," and it is her love of books that led to her degree in English literature. She resides in New York City and Connecticut.

JANET TAYLOR LISLE's enduring fascination with the nature of reality permeates her well-loved novels, among them *Forest, The Lampfish of Twill, The Great Dimpole Oak,* and *Afternoon of the Elves,* which received a Newbery Honor medal in 1990. Her newest work, *The Lost Flower Children,* was published by Philomel Books in the spring of 1999. She lives on the coast of Rhode Island. For more information on Janet, visit her website: *www.JanetTaylorLisle.com.*

RICHARD PECK is the author of the 1998 Newbery Honor book and National Book Award finalist *A Long Way from Chicago.* He has also written the favorites *The Great Interactive Dream Machine; Ghosts I Have Been,* named by the American Library Association as one of the Best of the Best Book Books for Young Adults; and *Father Figure,* an ALA Best Book for Young Adults. Richard has received several awards for the body of his work, including the 1990 Margaret A. Edwards Award and the 1997 Empire State Award, and is a two-time recipient of the Edgar Allen Poe Award for Best Young Adult Mystery. His newest book, *Amanda-Miranda,* is condensed from its adult form for young readers, and he is currently working on a sequel to *A Long Way from Chicago,* which will be released in the summer of 2000. He lives in New York City.

NANCY SPRINGER's diverse books have won her fans both old and young. She is a two-time recipient of the Edgar Allen Poe Award for Best Young Adult Mystery, first for *Toughing It* and then for *Looking for Jamie Bridger.* Her most recent novel for young readers, *I am Mordred: A Tale from Camelot,* was named a Best Book for Young Adults by the American Library Association. She is currently working on a follow-up entitled *I am Morgan le Fay,* as well as an anthology of original stories about frogs called *Ribbiting Tales.* She lives in Dallastown, Pennsylvania.

RITA WILLIAMS-GARCIA is the author of *Blue Tights, Fast Talk on a Slow Track,* and *Like Sisters on the Homefront,* the last a 1996 Coretta Scott King Honor Book that will air on Showtime as a television movie. She has also contributed to three previous anthologies of original fiction: *Join In: Multiethnic Short Stories by Outstanding Writers for Young Adults,* edited by Donald R. Gallo; *Trapped! Cages of Mind and Body,* edited by Lois Duncan; and *Dirty Laundry: Stories About Family Secrets,* edited by Lisa Rowe Fraustino. Her latest novel, *Every Time a Rainbow Dies,* will be published in 2001. She is the mother of two daughters and lives in Queens, New York.